A LIGHT
IN A WORLD OF
DARKNESS

A LIGHT
IN A WORLD OF
DARKNESS

PAUL GARDINER

ARCHWAY
PUBLISHING

Archway Publishing books may be ordered through booksellers or by contacting:

Archway Publishing
1663 Liberty Drive
Bloomington, IN 47403
www.archwaypublishing.com
1-(888)-242-5904

This is a work of fiction. All of the characters, names, incidents,
organizations, and dialogue in this novel are either the products
of the author's imagination or are used fictitiously.

ISBN: 978-1-4808-0674-0 (sc)
ISBN: 978-1-4808-0675-7 (e)

Library of Congress Control Number: 2014905809

Printed in the United States of America

Archway Publishing rev. date: 04/01/2014

THE WEDDING

On the night of January 1, 2015 a wedding was being held at a reception hall in western Maryland. The twenty-four year old bride, Karina Foster, wore a white wedding gown with flowers cut out throughout the train and a pink flower in her hair. The twenty-seven year old groom, Michael Essential, wore a tuxedo. After Karina and Michael said, "I do," and kissed, Michael's father and mother, John and Trisha looked at each, other and said in unison, "Finally," as the crowd of two hundred people cheered.

CHAPTER 1

John remembered 2012, when Michael first brought Karina home for dinner. Trisha opened the door and was shocked to see how young and beautiful she was. Karina had dark black hair, cat-like-eyes, and a tan from spending time at the beach. Michael, on the other hand, was an even 6 feet tall and weighed 160 pounds. He had black hair and green eyes.

Michael's life until that point had followed a similar path to other young men his age. He was a failure and a loner who could not catch a break. He had only one relationship with a women who, who later cheated on him and lied about it twice. As a result, he was cautious when it came to meeting a women and starting a relationship. Michael would not deal with people who caused other people problems whether it was a person at his job or a woman. Watching other people make mistakes in their relationship a lot; he always tried to learn from those mistakes. He could not stand lying, cheating, and stealing, especially the lying. Over time, he became more and more introverted as people used him. Women would use him for money or as an emotional crutch. They dumped their problems on Michael until they found someone better. Then they left.

Employers would say this will never happen at a job and that one event they said would not happen did. Michael had a bachelor's degree in exercise science, but did not want to be a physical education teacher. So he started moving to different areas of the United States. However, most of the places he worked did not have job openings field related to his major and so he ended up taking jobs that were not in his field. In addition he faced high costs of living. At one point in his life, it got so bad that he applied to receive welfare in the state of North Carolina. However, the women at the welfare office told him that he had to have a child or custody of a child to receive any benefits other than emergency healthcare. Due to issues like these Michael would keep moving from state to state.

From dealing with these situations, Michael had finally learned an important rule of life; always look into everything before jumping into a situation, and always look out for yourself. Others will not look out for you. If one does not look into the situation first, years of their life can be taken away from a person because they have dedicated them to fixing just one problem in their life, whether it is caused by themselves or others. However, Michael wrote a book made some money and bought an upscale restaurant. Now for the first time in his life, his world had changed for the better, but that was about to change once again.

While Karina and Michael ate dinner, John and Trisha pounded them with questions, particularly about how they met. Michael answered, "We met on a mission trip to Costa Rica. Karina was there as a youth group leader for her church, and so was I." We exchanged numbers and started dating regularly when we got back to the States.

Later on that night, Michael and his father watched their favorite baseball team sweep another team, Trisha and Karina were sat at the dinner table, drinking coffee. Trisha, who didn't want to see her son hurt again, asked Karina what she liked about Michael.

Karina said, "I think Michael is good-looking, but what I liked most about him was that he was different from other men I had dated. Most guys lied to me or talked about sex constantly. Michael did not. That is what makes our relationship work."

PRESENT

The wedding party was leaving and heading to the banquet hall. While, they were leaving, the caterers were putting the finishing touches on the tables in the wedding hall. One woman was walking around, lighting all the candles at the tables, while Paul was pouring champagne.

Paul was an absolute failure-just like Michael was. Up to this point, he had moved to several states, working two or, sometimes three jobs to make ends meet and had to pay off $20,000 in college debt. Paul loved his new job, though. Working as a caterer was easy. The company's owners gave him excellent health benefits, two weeks of paid vacation, and a 401 K plan. He got free food as well. The other employees were also easy to work with, and he almost always met new people who were interesting. On top of all this, Paul was able to get a 2007 Lamborghini with the money he had saved up from doing lawn care and painting murals for businesses. For the first time in his life everything was just fine, He still thought he should have gone to a culinary arts school in Pennsylvania, where he grew up. Anything would have been better than going to a regular four year college and getting a degree in political science. At this stage in his life, Paul wondered, why parents push their high school kids to go to college, telling them they would find a job, even if it is not in their major. Paul knew that only 20 percent of students even get a job in their major after they graduate. Trade schools are where it's at, he thought to himself.

When the bride and groom finally walked in to the banquet hall Karina mentioned to Michael how beautiful the hall was. The hall had crystal chandeliers, new hardwood flooring, a padded bar with free drinks for the guests, and all the walls were mirrors. When the newlyweds sat down, the best man and the maid of honor gave their toasts. Then the pastor gave the prayer, and the caterers started serving food. Finally, when everyone was served, the forks started hitting the champagne glasses signaling for bride and groom to kiss.

As guests settled down to enjoy their dinners, Paul was going around serving more drinks. An attractive woman in her early twenties with long wavy black hair, brown eyes, and a beach tan, kept eyeing

Paul, she didn't say anything to him. Meanwhile, Paul is not notice her because there were so many attractive women there.

After, the parents and the best man gave their speeches, the bride and groom danced the first song. Slowly the dance floor started to fill up, according to the intoxication level of the people at the reception. The servers started to clear their tables until the catering manager told them take a break. Then Paul walked up to the bar to grab a drink. The women who had been watching him decided to get in line behind him. Paul did not notice her until she asked him how long he had been doing his job.

He said, "About nine months." She then asked how she could get a job with the caterer. He answered, "You could go to a culinary arts school and take hotel and restaurant management." After a slight pause he told her that he actually got lucky, and someone gave him a chance at this job. "God smiled upon me so I didn't have to pay for training at all."

Suddenly, their conversation was interrupted by the bar-tender, who asked Paul what he wanted. He asked for some hard liquor. Then the brown-eyed girl leaned up against the bar and said, "You really know how to get a party started don't ya?" A light went off in Paul's head, and he thought, "By the end of the night, this girl will be knocked on her rear by the alcohol; not a good sign." Then he got his vodka and walked away.

Hours later the bridal bouquet garter were thrown. A blond, blue-eyed man, who was built like a football player, caught the garter and a tall blonde caught the bouquet-or tried to. Her eyes were as blue as her dress, which was covered in white flowers and had a slit up the side, exposing most of her well developed thigh. This dress also had a slit that led all the way up her leg exposing most of her thigh. Every man, as well as some of the woman in the room stared at her, including the jock that caught the garter. Some of the women even had a look of disgust on their faces. However, as fate would have it, the blonde was heavily intoxicated. She staggered and dropped the bouquet into the hands of the attractive, dark-haired woman who had been talking to Paul.

Paul had been standing along the wall with the rest of the servers, watching the whole scene unfold. Then he started to laugh, as the smile on the blond, hair blue-eyed guy's face slowly faded. By just looking at the way the blond man acted Paul new the guy really wanted the blond to catch the bouquet and not the dark haired women. He also knew that the guy was probably one of those jerks who only goes for the best looking woman in the crowd and just uses her as if she is a sex object to him.

After the dark-haired woman sat down on the chair, the music started playing. Then the blond man put the garter on the woman's leg, while she was watching Paul. Then everyone clapped and started dancing again.

Later on while everyone was still dancing the blond hair guy started dancing with the blond woman and grabbed her rear. She slapped, him pushed him away, and sat back down in her seat. Then the blond guy called her a female dog and sat down in his seat. Paul saw this and about ten minutes later he dropped one of the wine glasses off the tray he was carrying to the dishwasher into the jerks lap. He told the man he was sorry and tried to clean it up but the man told him that he had done enough damage and to leave. Paul continued walking to the kitchen and dropped his glasses off for the dishwashers to wash with a grin on his face.

When Paul went out to collect more dishes he walked through the dance floor and by the dark haired woman's table. Seeing this as her chance she took the opportunity to dance with him by walking up to him and started grinding up against him on the dance floor. Paul caved in and danced with her for the whole song. Finally, when the song was over he said, "You do not give up easily do you?" They exchanged numbers and he left to finish cleaning up the dishes. While this was all going on the blond loser saw this as an opportunity to get back at Paul for the embarrassment he caused him earlier.

After Paul left the room the blond haired piece of white trash walked up to the black haired women and asked her to dance. She said, "No." He said, "Come on, let's dance then I will take you home and you can show me if you are as nasty in the bed as you are on the dance floor." She then slapped him in the face and told him to get lost.

After that the dark haired woman had had enough of the wedding and wanted to go home. She then called Paul. Paul answered his phone saying, "Who is this?" She said, "Deseray, could you walk me out to my car? That jerk tried to dance with me. I said no and he harassed me. " Paul replied, "I will be there in a minute." Then Paul asked the manager in charge if he could leave and that it was an emergency he had to go deal with it. The manager said, "Yes." Then Paul and Deseray left the building.

On the way out to the car the blond haired man walked out of an alley and punched Paul in the face. Then he elbowed Paul in the face. Paul fell to the ground and the guy tried to pull Deseray into the alley but she kicked him in his mid-section. The guy then slapped her in the face making Deseray bleed. Paul got up hit him in the face and broke his nose making blood fly everywhere. The guy tried to fight back but Paul kicked him in the stomach and the guy threw up beer all over himself. Paul threw him to the ground and punched him in the head till he was unconscious. Paul looked at Deseray while asking if she was ok. She said, "Yes." Then he said, "You know what we should do?" "What is that," she said? "Let's put this white trash where he belongs, in the dumpster so grab his feet and I will grab his arms." Then they both threw him in the dumpster and called the police. Paul told the police that the blond man was in the dumpster and to meet them at the bar so they could give their side of the story.

After that they walked to the bar and had a drink to help with the pain. When the police officers got there they told Paul and Deseray that they could not find the blond hair man. Deseray said, "Next time I see him again he will not be so lucky." Then Paul and Deseray gave their description of the blond man. When the officers were finished Paul and Deseray both drove to the hospital.

When Paul was finished getting the cut above his eye sown up and Deseray got the cut on her lip sown up. They walked out to the parking lot hugged each other good bye because of Deseray's swollen lip and went home.

CHAPTER 2

The Honeymoon

Michael and Karina went on their honeymoon to northeast North Carolina staying at their Uncle Lieberum's beach house for free. Uncle Lieberum fought in Vietnam as a Marine and after his four years was up he came home. Then he got a job as a government contractor, worked for forty years and retired. That is how he was able to afford his beach house. He also had a wife named Janet.

Janet had blond hair blue eyes and was forty years old but she looked like she was thirty. Uncle Lieberum had brown hair, brown eyes, and rough features. His wife liked him because he was funny, laid back, level headed, a good cook, and always calm under pressure.

Michael was their favorite nephew. He always treated everyone with respect and gave everyone the credit they deserved. The other nephew's name was not even worth mentioning. He was an alcoholic, who despite many tries could not quit drinking so because of Michael's good character he was able to use the beach house as a wedding gift.

Two days after their wedding Karina and Michael woke up early to go to a church in the Outer Banks. Before church they meet with

Janet and Uncle Lieberum for breakfast at a local restaurant. When the newlyweds walked in Uncle Lieberum was reading a newspaper. On the front page the headlines read, "American Journalist Killed In Dubai." The police investigation turned up no clues or motive and the CIA was totally dumbfounded because they had no answers either, only suspicions.

At the restaurant the newlyweds and the Lieberums both decided to eat from the buffet. The buffet had everything a person could want from waffles, to fruits, ice tea, milk shakes, pancakes, French toast, sausage, ham and steak; the list goes on. On top of all this, there was a great view of the ocean and the food was free because the owner let them have it as a wedding gift. When they were finished both families went to church together.

In church the Pastor talked about John 3:16-21. It states:

"16. For God so loved the world that he gave his only son, that whoever believes in him shall not perish but have eternal life. 17. For God did not send his only son into the world to condemn the world, but to save the world through him. 18. Whoever believes in him is not condemned, but whoever does not believe stands condemned already because he has not believed in the name of God's one and only son. 19. This is the verdict: Light has come into the world, but men loved darkness instead of light because their deeds were evil. 20. Everyone who does evil hates the light, and will not come into the light in fear that his deeds will be exposed. 21. But whoever lives by the truth comes into the light, so that it will be seen plainly that what he has done has been done through God (NIV)."

The Pastor then goes on to explain the meaning of the passage verse by verse. "3:16 means exactly what it says. Verse 17 means that the Law of Moses or the Ten Commandments condemn so that sacrifices of lambs and goats are not needs anymore just faith in Christ. However, Christ is not here to get rid of the Ten Commandments because they are written in love and to glorify God showing his grace. Verse 18 shows that Christ is the only way to heaven because the Father, Son, and the wholly spirit are one in the same and are the trinity. Good works does not mean you go to heaven. Even Hitler did good works at some point. Verse 19 tells us that mankind has a natural tendency towards evil. Verses 20-21 Evil does its work in the darkness of night or does what everyone wants to see and hear in the light. However, everything it does even if it happens to do good is done with a concealed motive that is meant for selfish interests. For instance, I do something nice to gain a person's confidence then when they let their guard down I rob them blind. See, everything an evil person does is a calculated plot to get what they want and some do not even know they are doing it. In other words everything evil does is selfish or self-seeking."

"What is the truth we speak about in verse 21," the pastor said. "Well the bible tells use the answer to this in James 1:27," according to the pastor. This passage states; "Religion that God our father accepts as pure and faultless is this: to look after orphans and widows in their distress and to keep oneself from being polluted by the world." "Well this is not hard most would think but they are wrong. John 15 tells us what to expect." Verse 20 through 21 says, [20] "Remember what I told you: 'A servant is not greater than his master.'[b] If they persecuted me, they will persecute you also. If they obeyed my teaching, they will obey yours also. [21] They will treat you this way because of my name, for they do not know the one who sent me. [22] If I had not come and spoken to them, they would not be guilty of sin; but now they have no excuse for their sin. [23] Whoever hates me hates my Father as well. [24] If I had not done among them the works no one else did, they would not be guilty of sin. As it is, they have seen, and yet they have hated both me and my Father. [25] But this is to fulfill what is written in their Law: 'They hated me without reason (NIV)."

"However, do not get discouraged John 14:1-4 gives us an encouraging word. "Do not let your hearts be troubled. You believe in God; believe also in me. [2] My Father's house has many rooms; if that were not so, would I have told you that I am going there to prepare a place for you? [3] And if I go and prepare a place for you, I will come back and take you to be with me that you also may be where I am. [4] You know the way to the place where I am going (NIV)."

"In this passage Jesus is not just talking to the disciples he is talking about all of us. Jesus says that by following me you will not be forgotten and I am the only way to the father. Therefore, by following these words that I have given you there will be a great reward for you. Whether it is here on earth now or in heaven and maybe even both, that is for you to decide. The pastor then said, "Amen." Then he asked for all who wanted to receive Christ into their hearts to come up to the alter to receive him."

When Essentials and Lieberums left the church they discussed meeting for dinner later that night at the beach house. Michael said, "How about a cook out?" "Sure," said John Lieberum. "I will bring desert. You guys get the food," John added. Then both families went their separate ways.

On the way back to the hotel John and Janet stayed at for the weekend, they talked about Karina. "What do you think about Karina," said Janet? "She seems like a nice girl," said John. Then John said, "What do you think?" "She is beautiful and I am just glad he is not all shy as well as, depressed like he used to be," said Janet. "Lunch," said John. "Yes! Good timing. I was just about to ask you myself," said Janet. Then John pulled the convertible into the parking lot of a seafood/Café restaurant. The café had a beautiful view of the ocean and they cooked the food right in front of the customers.

John ordered the ribs, shrimp, and a baked potato with sour cream, while Janet had a club sandwich with some fries. John had wine with his meal and Janet had a soda. Then they discussed what they should get for a desert for that night. When the waitress heard the word desert she came right over and asked, "Would the young couple like desert?" Janet cracked a smile John did not say anything. Then Janet replied, "No thanks we were just talking about the young couple we are eating dinner with tonight. They just got married and are going to have a cookout. We told them we would bring desert." The waitress replied, "I have just the thing, hold on."

The waitress disappeared and came back with a black forest cake. "Nice! How much is it," said John? "The whole cake is usually $20.00 dollars but we will give it to you for half." "Sold," said John? After paying the bill the Lieburums left.

On the way out of the restaurant Janet said, "John lets go to a grocery store." For what reason would that be," said John? "You will see," said Janet. As they drove down the road a delivery boy drove past them and cut them off because he was late for a delivery. John said, "He is going to cause an accident. I hate it when people do not think of other people and do what they want. They will not figure out what they do wrong until someone gets killed or they go to jail. Sometimes they are just too stupid to figure it out at all." Then John and Janet pulled into a grocery store.

While Mrs. Lieberum was in the grocery store the pizza delivery boy pulled up to a beach house and knocked on a door. The door opened and Michael Essential stepped out. "$12.39," the pizza boy said. Then Michael handed him a twenty and said, "Keep the change." The delivery boy handed him the package and left. Michael took the package outside to the table on the back porch. Then he walked all the way to the water and yelled to Karina which had swum a quarter mile out into the ocean that the food was here. After telling Karina about the food Michael then walked back into the beach house and poured Karina's favorite drink into a cup called "Cloud Surfers: Number Nine." "Cloud Surfers" was a new none alcoholic mixed drink. This drink was a milk shake that tasted like hard liquor mixed with grape soda, and vanilla ice cream. Michael poured himself a soda.

By the time Michael was finished pouring the drink and walked back out to the porch. Karina walked up the stairs drying her body off with a towel. Then she sat down at the table on the back porch to eat the Stromboli Michael cut in half. While they were eating Michael asked, "Karina, how did you get in so fast?" "I rode the wave in," she said. Michael laughed as some of the sauce from the Stromboli dripped down her neck and in between her breasts. Karina said, "I am such a mess. Pass me a napkin." Michael answered, "I have a better idea." Then he walked over to Karina and licked the sauce off of her. She laughed and put her arms around him. Then he picked her up saying, "This food is for the birds." Then he carried her inside to the bedroom.

Meanwhile, John was waiting outside the grocery store for Janet when he heard a scream. He looked around to see where the sound was coming from. Upon not see where it was coming from he ignored it. Then he heard it again. There was a girl drowning out in the water. John swam out there to save her. Then he brought her back onto the beach to administer rescue breathing. Just then Janet walked out to the car with some cheese, a stick of meat and a bottle of champagne in a bag. Noticing that her husband was not there she threw the champagne in the car and looked up to see all the commotion that was going on. Then she ran to where her husband was administering rescue breathing, pulled her phone out and called 911.

Back at the beach house Michael walked out of the bedroom. After having skipped the main course and going straight to desert Michael was hungry. He walked out on the porch to find nothing on the table as Karina walked out of the bedroom putting her bathing suit top back on. Michael looked along the beach to find the brown paper bag the Stromboli came in blowing around in the wind. Then Karina and Michael look up to see two seagulls fighting in midair over the Stromboli. They were both latched onto it by their feet. Karina says, "I am betting on the one on the right with the oddly shaped beak. Whoever's seagull wins gets to pick the restaurant for dinner tomorrow." Michael replied, "Deal!"

Neither one of the seagulls could overtake the other for several minutes. There were feathers falling out of the sky everywhere. Michael was filming the whole fight on his phone because it looked like a pillow fight in the sky with all the feathers of the two seagulls falling to the ground. Then suddenly the normal seagull was able to peck off part of the wing of the seagull with the odd beak and they both went crashing down to the ground. There was no movement for a second leaving both Michael and Karina wondering what happened. "Looks like the one seagull was too stupid to let go of the Stromboli letting gravity do the rest. Now they are both knocked out. Look! Now no one goes home with the Stromboli. Maybe they should have used some bipartisanship and split the Stromboli." Karina laughed and said, "How do you expect two seagulls to do that when humans cannot?" Michael started to laugh saying, "Good point but there is nothing to see here now." Then the two of them started to walk back into the beach house.

Suddenly, the seagull with the strange beak started to wake up and slowly make its way toward the Stromboli. However, the other seagull woke up and took flight grabbing the Stromboli with its feet. Then it started flying away from shore towards a boat about a half a mile away. By this time both Michael and Karina turned around to see what was going on. Michael started to smile thinking he had won the bet as the injured seagull took flight. However, at about a quart mile away from the boat the seagull with the odd beak and now an injured wing caught up to as well as grabbed the other seagulls foot with his beak. The other seagull instantly fell from the sky dropping the Stromboli into the water. The strange beak seagull then dived into the water, picked up the Stromboli, and flew back to shore.

At the same time this was happening, the normal seagull was flailing in the water, blood leaking from his foot. A fin came up out of the water circling around the seagull. Michael and Karina turned around to see the oddly beaked bird enjoying their Stromboli on the table behind them. Then they turned back around to see no more seagull or shark in the water only blood. Where do you want to go to eat," said Michael. "I do not know. Let's go for a ride and see," said Karina.

Later, when Michael and Karina were done looking at a Peruvian restaurant they would eat at the next day, Michael sat down to read a book while Karina went out to tan. They were doing these activities to burn time till the Lieberum's got there. While Michael and Karina were relaxing an ambulance finally came and got the little girl Mr. Lieburum had saved. The Lieburums answered the police's questions. Then they left for the Essential's beach house for dinner.

When the Lieburums showed up Karina and Michael were surprised to see them walking in with a black forest cake, some champagne, cheese, and a stick of meat. Michael and John went out on the porch to cook some hamburgers, while the women sat down talking about the fight outside the wedding banquet.

"Did you know there was a fight outside your wedding banquet," said Janet? "No, I did not," said Karina. Janet replied, "Deseray (a friend of the family) and some caterer went outside and Jake that was a friend of Michaels in high school had a fight over her. Jake lost and was thrown in a trash dumpster." "I will have to call her," said Karina. Just then, John and Michael walked in and Michael said, "Dinner is ready." The women set the table. Everyone sat down and prayed. Then they ate dinner.

After a delicious dinner, Michael and John did the dishes then the women served the desert. The desert was wonderful and everyone talked about the wedding. Finally, after some champagne the Lieburums spent the night and went back to Maryland the next morning.

CHAPTER 3

The Perfect Day And A
Night to Remember

STILL IN THE PAST

Deseray talked about the wedding and how she knew Karina, while walking through a park in south eastern Pennsylvania with Paul. She also told Paul that they were friends since their freshmen year of college. They both swam on the same college team and that is how they meet. Paul asked how did Karina meet Michael and she told him how they meet on a missions trip.

After a while of hearing Deseray talk about funny and embarrassing events that happened to her and Karina in college Paul decided to ask a question to change the conversation. "Want to see a good view," Paul said? "Yes sure," said Deseray. "Let's go to the car," said Paul.

Meanwhile, Karina and Michael were finishing their honeymoon on the coast of North Carolina. They were driving down to check out an historical southern town on the ocean, when they were cut off by another driver who hit the car right beside them sending the other car flipping off the bridge into the inlet below. "I better call the emergency services," said Karina. Then she dialed 911. After that they got to their destination and went for a walk on the boardwalk.

Back in Pennsylvania the car Paul and Deseray were in crept up the hill to a picnic area with an overlook. They got out and walked to the edge to see out over a cliff that gives you a beautiful view of the Susquehanna River. "What a beautiful view Paul. You can see for miles," said Deseray. "I like seeing how green all the trees are and the eagles that fly around here most the time. There is also a five mile hiking path that goes down through the woods and has some water crossings. However, the day is getting late and maybe we should go eat lunch, but first." After a short pause Deseray replied, "Yes Paul." Then Paul and Deseray kissed.

While, Paul and Deseray were taking advantage of the view then heading to lunch, John and Janet were heading up 301 through Virginia to avoid traffic on Interstate 95. "Man this drive is so boring," said John. "You want me to drive for a while," said Janet? "No, it is just so mundane," replied John. "Well in an hour or two we can sit and eat here in Virginia. Then go horseback riding, drive another hour get some Chesapeake Bay crabs in Maryland, (not the fake junk they got in some town that says they are from the Chesapeake but are from Alaska) and drive back eight or nine o'clock at night. This will help us avoid the traffic on interstate 95," said Janet. "That sounds like a good plan," replied John.

After their walk Karina and Michael walked into a seafood restaurant. The host sat them outside on the porch to enjoy the cool wind that was blowing and the view of the sea. Then the waitress came and asked them what they wanted. They asked for some water then went ahead and ordered some calamari as an appetizer. "Wouldn't this be a great place to live," asked Karina? "Yes, it would but I need to get the chain of restaurants going up north first just in case before we move down here and the economy falls apart. Otherwise if this does not work I have something to fall back on other than just writing books," Michael said.

Just then the waitress retuned with some water and asked, "What would you like as an entrée?" "We would both like a wrap. We are not interested in dinner just lunch," answered Karina. What type of wrap would you like said, the waitress. "I would like the chicken Caesar wrap with tuna fish in it," replied Karina. Then Michael answered, "The same wrap with Catalina dressing instead of tuna. The waitress replied, "I will put in your order and the Calamari should be done by now so I should be right back with your appetizer." Then she walked to the kitchen to check on their food.

In the meantime, Paul's sports car pulled into a small restaurant that specialized in homegrown foods produced by the Amish. Just then Deseray noticed the horse and buggy parked a crossed the parking lot. "That horse looks so beautiful Paul. It would be great if I could afford one day," said Deseray. "I do not know if you would like dealing with the smell of dung all day long. Having worked on a horse farm before, I should know. The smell was horrible and so were the flies. One of the horses would always be trying to steal my equipment from me," replied Paul. Deseray laughed and said, "You have bad luck with animals don't you? Then she paused and said, "I remember the story you told me about the first time your friend introduced you to their dog named Peppy."

THE STORY

Paul woke up one morning in college to a phone call from his friend Derick. "You coming over to watch my cat and puppy while I am gone for the day," said Derick. "Sure," said Paul. When Paul pulled up to the house there was a dead rabbit laying on the front door step. Paul walked up to the door knocked and Derick answered. "I guess someone left you a surprise," said Paul with a smile? Then Derick replied, "That cat, I cannot stand it. The cat eats grass all the time so it can puke everywhere and claws up everything as well. On top of that the cat was infested with heart worms when we first got it, (which were expensive to get rid of) and as you can see the cat likes to bring us little presents as well." "Well, what did you expect? You know my theory. If God created them outside they should stay out there where they belong," said Paul with a smile.

After a pause, Derick said, "If you get sick of them put them outback where there is a fence and they cannot get out. The dog has a hemp rope he likes to chew on. If he starts to chew on anything get the hemp rope out and let him chew on that instead. Like I said, if they both become too bad just put them out in the back yard, but do not let the cat get out the front door or he will knock boots with the other cats in town." "What is wrong Derick. Wife not letting you have any because you're not performing well in bed? That does not mean you have to take it out on the cat," replied Paul as he starts to laugh. "No, the neighbors are threatening to sue because they have pure breed Persian cats that compete in competitions. They do not want any **"impurities"** in the family line, as they like to say," said Derick. "Russian Blues and a Persian Kitten mix! I want to see that. Headlines would read, "Persian Kitten with the Russian Blues," sounds like a cat with a new disease to me," replied Paul. "Seriously, my wife does not want to neuter or declaw the cat. She would kill me if we had to do that. The only reason we have this cat is because my wife is allergic to cat hair and Russian Blues have very short hair that does not fly everywhere," said Derick.

Paul began to laugh and said, "Nothing is funnier than reality. You just cannot write this stuff. You wife is a vegan who gives money to an animal rights activist group and you are an active member of a national gun advocate group. Tell me where does this make any sense at all Derick or is it love concerns all? The biggest lie ever."

Derick laughed and went out to go hunting. Paul went and feed the cat outside on the back porch. Then he went inside to feed the dog that by this time had a hold of a pillow. Paul tried to pull it away from the puppy but it was no use because it was a baby pit-bull terrier named Peppy and it was not letting go. Then Paul thought I should go and get the hemp rope, get him to grab it, and pull him outside.

Paul grabbed a hold of the hemp rope that was on the coffee table next to some glue and glitter that Derick's wife Shawna was using to make crafts because she was a school teacher. The puppy saw this and ran up to the hemp rope grabbing a hold of it. Paul started pulling the dog towards the door and slipped falling onto the coffee table getting glue all over the back of him. Then the puppy dropped the rope in the middle of the floor and barked at Paul daring him to go get the hemp rope. Paul says, "All right I will play your game," Paul said diving for the rope. They both got hold of it at the same time while sliding across the floor and into the wall effectively knocking them out.

Two hours later Paul woke up with a splitting headache and the smell of dog urine that was all over him. Paul looked for the rope and found it glued to his rear end. After that he began to look around the room but there was no dog there so Paul started to go upstairs. When he turned around the corner towards Derick and his wife Shawna's room he saw the puppy had torn up the sheets to the bed. Paul yelled, "They are going to neuter you for sure now!" Then the dog ran down the stairs and towards the back window diving for it. However, Paul chased after him and dived also but not at the right angle and hit his stomach on the window sill. Trying to get himself up he accidently grabbed the cat that was eating below the sill and the cat wrapped his claws around Paul's hand and started biting him. Paul tried to pull his arm back but the cat was firmly latched to him so he swung the cat into the window about five times trying to get the cat off of him only to have the window fall on him hurting him. Leaving his rear with the rope still glued to it exposed to the puppy who came back in the house through the doggy door to the back yard. Paul hit the cat up against the glass of the window one final time breaking the glass and knocking the cat out. Then the puppy missed biting the rope glued to Paul's rear and bit Paul's rear instead. Paul screams in pain then wraps his legs around the puppy's neck till he let go.

Finally, Paul pulls the rope off of him and throws it out window watching the dog go after it. Then Paul walks gingerly out the door he picks up the passed out cat and throws the cat in his cage, while locking the door to the cage. Paul picks up a milk bone and throws it into the puppy's cage. The puppy ran after it and fell victim to Paul's trick as Paul locked the cage door behind him. Then Paul said, "Before I make a trip to the hospital I got one more trick just wait till the cat wakes up."

TEN MINUTES LATER

Opening his eyes the cat screeched in horror as Paul dumped a bucket of soap and water on both the dog and the cat. Paul then started spraying them with the hose laughing while the cat put its claws around the gate to the cage. When Paul was done spraying the dog was huddled up in the corner of the cage whimpering while the cat had a death grip with his claws on the cage door. The cat was breathing heavy, heart pumping fast, and looking like a wet rat. After that Paul called Derick and told him what happened. Paul then went to the hospital. When Derick got home he told the puppy that he expected this from him but the cat was too old to be acting like this, so Derick took the cat cage to the front porch and opened it so the cat could go get in trouble throughout the town.

"I still have bit marks on my rear from that dog," said Paul to Deseray. Deseray walked up slapped him in the rear laughing and said, "You will have to show me those scars sometime." Then they walked in the restaurant.

FIVE MINUTES LATER

Immediately, as soon as the door opened to the restaurant, the host asked, "Would you like a booth or a table?" Deseray answered, "A booth." After that the waitress sat the menus on the table and asked what drink they would like. Paul and Deseray both said, "Soda." Then the waitress left to go get the drinks.

In the meantime, Deseray and Paul looked at the menu and decided what they wanted. When the waitress came back she asked, "Would you like something off the menu or the buffet?" They both answered, "Buffet." After that Paul and Deseray walked up to the buffet to check it out. The buffet had the classic Amish foods to feast on. One of the foods was Bova Shankel that was dumplings that looked like pirogues, with a buttery sauce on top of it. Another one was shoo fly pie and finally Schnitz Un Knepp, which has dumplings, apple, and ham in it. Needless to say after a half an hour of straight eating food they were both stuffed.

Later on, that night Deseray and Paul walked into a local night club and sat down at a booth. At the same time they walked in two men in trench coats walked up behind a guy down the street, grabbed him and pulled him into an alley. The two goons told him to give them his wallet. He handed the wallet to them and they looked through it to find a single hundred dollar bill. "This should be enough," said the one goon. Then the other knocked him out with chloroform.

When the man woke up he felt something slippery that was clenched in his hands and noticed he was chained to a medical examiners table. He looked at his hands closely again and tried to scream but he could not because he had his vocal cords in his hands.

Back at the club Paul ordered some rum and Deseray ordered an Irish car bomb. They also ordered a sampler with wings, quesadeas, shrimp, and a small amount of ribs. At the same time Jake was sitting at the bar getting wasted. He felt horrible about what he did at the wedding banquet and wanted to make it up to them but he did not see that Paul and Deseray were there so he just kept drinking. Jake then headed to the bathroom to vomit then started to leave.

However, later when he saw Paul and Deseray receiving their food from the waiter he told the bartender that he was going to pay for their food and drinks. After the waiter was told about the drinks being on Jake's tab he returned to see how Paul and Deseray were doing with their food. She told them that some guy had decided to pay for their meal and their drinks. Paul got up and went over to the guy to tell him thanks. When the guy turned around Paul immediately said, "What are you doing here jerk?" "This is my favorite night club and you just happened to be here. When I saw you I decided that I should make up for what I did. I am sorry I am a bad drunk," replied Jake. "Well do not say you are sorry to me but tell Deseray that," said Paul!

Jake walked over to the table with Paul and told Deseray that he was sorry and he was a bad drunk. The she forgave him and he left. Deseray turned to Paul and said, "Strange town don't you think." Paul then hugged her and gave her a kiss. Then they left the club.

On the way out they walked past the same alley the goons grabbed the man with no vocal cords. Then someone in a black jumpsuit with black gloves and a ski mask on grabbed Deseray and pulled her into the alley. Paul ran into the alley after the masked assailant and grabbed a metal pipe lying on the ground. The goon then threw Deseray into the brick wall head first knocking her unconscious. Paul then swung the metal pipe at the attacker but the assailant dived out of the way and counter attacked with a knee shattering kick. Paul fell helpless to the ground dropping the metal pipe. The masked assailant picked up the pipe and swung the pipe straight into Paul's face sending blood splattering everywhere, breaking Paul's jaw. The attacker then dragged Paul to a trash dumpster stacked some wooden crates up and dragged Paul to the top of the crates. Then he tied Paul to the dumpster and with his neck hanging over the edge of the dumpster. While this was going on Deseray started to come too. The assailant climbed on top of the dumpster grabbed the metal lid and jumped off grabbing the metal lid and slamming it on Paul's neck breaking his neck. Then Deseray seeing Paul's neck being broken yelled, "Paul!" and passed out as the murder looked into her eyes.

CHAPTER 4

No Evidence Just Bad Memories

PRESENT

Deseray's concentrating was exceptional as she pulled the trigger to let the bullet out of the chamber. The bullet hit the target right in the center circle. After the shooting range was clear the range workers went and got their targets. Then Deseray went and sat down next to her dad as the range workers tallied the contestant's scores. "Honey how do you think you did today," said her dad? "I do not know Marc we will see," said Deseray?

Finally, the scores were in and Deseray had yet again won a shooting competition. Hitting the target right in the center circle all but one time was all she needed to win yet another handgun tournament, her fourth one in five months. She accepted her prize of $4,000 dollars and her dad drove her to lunch at a German restaurant in western Maryland. When they sat down at the table the waitress asked what they would like to drink. They both said, "Water," and started looking at the menu as the waitress left to get their drinks.

When the waitress came back Marc ordered sausage bits with barbeque and pineapple. She ordered some beef stroganoff. They also both got the soup of the day which came with rye bread as their appetizer. When the waitress left to go get their appetizers Marc asked Deseray, "Are you ok?" She answered, "Just fine." Then she asked to be excused from the table. Went to the bathroom and started to cry.

When Deseray returned to the table the food was already on the table and Marc had started to eat. He knew something was wrong but decided to finish eating and talk about it later. There was not much conversation, just a few statements on how good the food was and some small talk. They did not eat desert, tipped the waitress, and left.

In the car on the way home to Pennsylvania they had a conversation on Deseray's work as a high school teacher. "How are the students doing on their tests," said Marc? "Some of them are going to fail and be held back next year but most of them will pass. I wish it was the old days when students got graded by the teachers. If they failed their assignments and tests they did not pass. None this teaching to the math, writing, or a reading test and if they fail the state test, they fail the year. I hate it because there are children that just suck at tests but if you ask them to do something that is on that test or make something, they can do it. Failing a test does not mean you are a failure. That is bull crap. Furthermore, if a child keeps getting a math test each time how are they supposed to pass English or reading when they spend most their time studying math. On top of this they should lose points for attendance. That is life. If you show up late for work all the time what is going to happen," said Deseray. "You will get fired," answered Marc. "Why should we not take points off of their final grade for attendance or tardiness? That will get them ready for when they go do some real work," replied Deseray.

Most of the drive home was little conversations about small stuff and listening to the radio. However, about twenty minutes from Deseray's house her dad asked her what the problem really was. "I am having nightmares about Paul's death again," answered Deseray. "Look I know how much he meant to you but that was three months ago, start dating again. There are millions of other guys out there. Give them a chance. You cannot be bummed out for the rest of your life. That is not healthy," said Marc.

FLASHBACK

Marc was a detective and was not on the scene immediately that night of Paul's death because he had turned his beeper off and was sleeping in his house alone. In fact, he did not get up until another police officer knocked on his door and told him Paul was dead then he rushed to see his daughter in the hospital. At the hospital she was asleep so rather than wake her up he went to talk to one of the nurses.

Marc asked the nurse, "What is the damage to her?" The nurse answered, "Head drama from where she was thrown into a wall. We cleaned out the wound disinfected it and sowed it back up. She is going to be ok. I do not know when she can leave. You will have to ask the head nurse." Marc went over to the head nurses' station and asked, "My daughter's name is Deseray Skylark. When will she be released?" "Tomorrow afternoon after we do some test to make sure she does not have any side effects from the concussion," answered the head nurse. After a pause she said, "I heard what happened I hope that everything works out fine for you and your daughter. It is just sick what people will do these days." Rather than ask what happened Marc decided he would go to the crime scene to help out with the investigation and find out from the authorities.

Then Marc walked back to his daughter's room kissed her on the forehead and said, "Goodbye." However, before he could leave the room he noticed she woke up and started crying, I wonder if she remembers what happened, Marc thought to himself. Deseray said, "Dad, please do not tell me what I saw was true and that Paul is dead or was it all just a dream?" "Sorry Deseray I cannot," answered Marc and Deseray continued to cry. Marc turned away from Deseray and said, "I am going to the scene of the crime to find out who did this or do you want me to stay here?" asked Marc. "Go ahead but answer me one question first," said Deseray. "What is that," said her dad? "When will I get out of here," asked Deeseray? Tomorrow, if you do not have any side effects from the concussion." Then Marc headed off to the crime scene to find out what exactly happened.

Pulling up to the scene Marc noticed lights from the police cars flashing and a woman ran up to him as he got out of his car. She yelled, "My husband is missing! I was supposed to meet him and my friends here at the club but he never showed up. I called twice in the four hours we were there but he has not shown. Marc said, "Look I am writing this down but I cannot say this is a missing person's case unless he has been gone forty-eight hours."

Then Marc asked, "When did you notice he was missing. "We were supposed to meet each other around 8:00 PM. However, my friends and I stayed in wait till fifteen minutes ago." Marc looked at his watch and noticed that it was twelve o'clock. Then the middle aged women said, "I called at 9:00 PM when he did not call me. My friends said, "Maybe he was sick or had to stay late at work but give him the benefit of the doubt you do not want him to think you do not trust him do you? Then I decided to leave him alone," said the middle aged women.

"Ok then, now give me a name and number which we can contact you by," said Marc. The women gave him her number and told him her name was Jenny Minkinson. I have work to do here but if your husband does not show up for forty eight hours give us a call. Here is the number to my office."

After the women left Marc turned his attention to the crime scene which the body had been carted off of two hours before. On the wall he saw the word hypocrite written in blood. What in the world is going on here," he asked one of the officers working the crime scene? "We found the victim dead with his neck broken by the dumpster, while your daughter was lying unconscious with her head bleeding on the ground next to the wall where the assailant or assailants threw her head first into the wall. There was also a blood trail leading from the body to the dumpster and inside the dumpster as well," answered the officer. "Sounds like this person or people really mean business," replied Marc. "Looks like we might have a serial killer or killers on our hands," said the officer. "I hope not having one serial killer is challenging enough but two that would be scary," said Marc.

Early the next morning Marc woke up to go visit his daughter Deseray in the hospital. When he got there he saw Deseray dressed in her hospital gown ready to go to her tests. He asked her what had happened the night before and she remembered only parts of the tragic evening. Then she went for her tests and her dad assured her that he would stay for when she finished her tests.

While her dad was waiting for her to get out of the testing room his phone rang. On the other end was one of the crime lab technicians. The technician said, "Remember the women named Jenny Minkinson?" "Yes," Marc replied. "Well her husband was in the alley that night we checked for prints in the alley and found his on some pipes that was hanging on the wall in the alley," according to the technician. When I am done waiting to see the results of my daughter's tests, I will come check and see what is going on at the station," replied Marc. "Hope everything is fine and goes well with your daughter," replied the lab technician.

Marc waited an hour to see the results of his daughters test. When Deseray was cleared to leave she walked up to her dad and said, "I am cleared to go home. There are no side effects or anything. They just gave me some pills for the headache and that the pain should go away in a couple days." "Good let's go home," replied Marc.

Several hours went by and Marc left Deseray sound asleep in her bed at her house to go to the station. When he arrived the lab technician told him that there was a trace of medal piping that was in the blood written on the wall and that they may be able to find the pipe at the crime scene. Marc replied, "Well that is the best news I have heard all day."

Meanwhile, the Paul's killer was standing down at the edge of a dock in New York City throwing a medal pipe wrapped in plastic into the water below. Then the killer went home and burned the clothing that was used to do the crime the night before.

CHAPTER 5

A Funeral And Complications

PAST

Two days later at the funeral, Deseray stood there as a familiar face showed up. Deseray noticed as Jake walked to the burial site. The whole time Jake was walking to the site Deseray thought to herself that Jake was the killer. Jake matched the description of the killer that she gave to her dad yesterday. The description was around six feet three inches tall, weighing 210 pounds and was well built.

While Jake was walking up to the burial site the Pastor read the eulogy. Part of the pastor's eulogy was read from 2 Corinthians Chapter 5:1-10 in the bible. "[1] Now we know that if the earthly tent we live in is destroyed, we have a building from God, an eternal house in heaven, not built by human hands. [2] Meanwhile, we groan, longing to be clothed with our heavenly dwelling, [3] because we are clothed, we will not be found naked. [4] For while we are in this tent, we groan and are burdened, because we do not wish to be unclothed but to be clothed with our heavenly dwelling, so that what is mortal may be swallowed up by life.

[5] Now it is God who has made us for this very purpose and has given us the Spirit as a deposit, guaranteeing what is to come. (NKJV)"

"Therefore we are always confident and know as long as we are at home in the body we are away from the Lord. [7] We live by faith, not by sight. [8] We are confident, I say, and prefer to be away from the body or away from the body and at home with the Lord. [9] So we are making it our goal to please him, whether we are at home in the body or away from it. [10] For we must all appear before the judgment seat of Christ, that each one may receive what is due him for the things done while in the body, whether good or bad. (NKJV)"

After the eulogy, Paul's family threw the first shovel full of dirt onto the casket, Pastor Daryl dismissed them and they went out to eat at an Italian restaurant. Deseray sat next to her dad and asked him to have Jake checked out to see if he was the killer. Then everyone (including the Pastor) except for Jake toasted and ate all you can eat Lasagna with garlic bread, spaghetti, and pizza.

The next day Marc went to the police station to talk to the police chief about having Jake put under surveillance. The police chief asked, "For what reason?" "First, he had a fight with Paul at a wedding a couple weeks back. Secondly, he bought them some food and drinks for Deseray and Paul the night of the murder. Finally, he showed up to the funeral," said Marc. "Sounds like he is either really sorry or a psycho that likes to see the fruits of his labor so go ahead we will check him out," replied the police chief. Marc immediately walked over to his computer to run through Jake's credit card records to see if anything came up that the detectives working the case could work with.

In the mourning Jake showed up for work at a local fitness club called "John and David's Backbreakers." Backbreakers had a weight room, a racquetball room, a rock climbing wall, as well as a dancehall with a stage that was used as a night club till two in the morning on Friday's and the weekends. The room was also used to cater events for a hefty price. When one left the room the doors opened to a bar and a nice place to eat breakfast, lunch, and dinner. Finally, there is another room with an Olympic size swimming pool and a Jacuzzi.

Next door was a tanning facility with a masseuse that also offered acupuncture that was built after the fitness center and conveniently placed next to the fitness club under different ownership. The masseuse and the fitness club were also three miles from a golf club.

Being a manager there Jake had the special privilege of a free membership to the fitness club and all of the facilities except the restaurant. The memberships were $50.00 a month usually. However, today he could not enjoy these privileges because he had to conduct interviews for a new fitness instructor position.

Jake had about five interviews to conduct today and walked into the building in a hurry. He had five minutes before the first interview so he decided to ignore all the girls working behind the counter staring at him accept for one named Jane. "How are you doing today Jane," he said? "Up yours Jake," answered Jane. Jake followed behind Jane as she went into the room behind the counter. Jane turned around and asked, "What do you want!" He then grabbed the water bottle from her and sprayed her with it saying, "For you to cool off. Your attitude doesn't do anything good for the club." Then he laughed at her. Everyone behind the counter saw the scene also and laughed to. Then he walked into the interview room sitting down next to his assistant Brad.

"Did I hear an up yours from Jane again Jake," said Brad? "Yes. That and her screams from getting sprayed with a water bottle," Jake replied with a smirk on his face. Brad said, "Your such a jerk Jake," mocking Jane in a fake girly voice. Then they both laughed knowing that Jane had a thing for Jake and it was only a matter of time before Jake would seal the deal and decide to sleep with Jane knowing she would let him.

Now, Jake and Brad had been friends ever since Jake was hired as the manager of the fitness club. Brad was giving a promotion to assistant manager by Jake after Jake realized how hard of a worker he was. They would always go clubbing together and hit the beach every so often. Brad and Jake thought highly of each other. However, Brad never approved of how Jake treated women because Jake was a stud and he knew this so he took advantage of women. "One day Jake is going to push it too far and I am going to have to put an end to this problem," Brad thought to himself.

"The first of the applicants used to work at a fitness center in New York with a high volume of members. He moved here because he just got married. He has a degree in physical fitness," said Brad. "See this is why I keep you around. You are always scouting out ahead doing your homework," said Jake.

After that the first applicant walked in. His name was Josh. The first question he was asked was, what was the worst problem you dealt with at the fitness center? The man answered, "A man was not paying attention when he picked up the dumbbell and dropped one on his finger slicing the skin off part of the finger." "How did you deal with the problem?" I had someone call 911. I personally wrapped the finger while applying pressure and put the bandage around it to help stop the bleeding. Then I put the skin in ice so it could be preserved longer so the physician had more time to sow the skin back on," answered Josh. "Impressive," said Jake!

"How much do you pay," asked Josh? "I was paid fifteen dollars an hour because I was a manager in New York," Josh continued. "Cost of living must have been pretty high," said Brad. Yes it was, so how much do you pay," said Josh? "Twelve dollars an hour," replied Jake. "I just got married and she has two children. I need more money than that," said Josh. "Sorry sir, we cannot do that. Twelve dollars an hour is pretty good for a single person not to mention for a household with two people working in it, replied Brad. "She has no job and lives on welfare as well as food stamps how am I supposed to take care of her and the children," asked Josh? "Look this is all we can do for you so take it or leave it," answered Jake. "Ok then. You guys have a nice day," replied Josh. Then Josh shook their hands and walked out to his $80,000.00 car.

"I really wanted to higher that guy," said Jake. "Don't you just love it when people think with the wrong body part and throw common sense out the window," said Brad. "Yeah, he probably used to live in a $300,000 dollar home and just moved in to a $500,000 home (that if he would have looked around longer he would have found it for $300,000 instead) with a women that does not work. She probably has $600.000 clothes; bad credit because she bought her ex-boyfriend a car and that deadbeat got fired from his job for stealing. Therefore, he did not make payments. Then to top it all off he leaves her with the kids and does not pay child support so she cannot pay any bills, said Jake.

"Yes, Josh will probably try to get her to get out of the house and work so he will not have to work 60 hours a week. However, she will say, I want to stay home with the kids because I do not trust other people with the children. Even though we all know that she is the problem and odds are good that the children get corrupted by her. Finally, in the end he finds a nice, beautiful girl at work that actually cares about him and pays attention to him telling him he does a good job. Then he will go home to hear his lazy wife complaining to him and he will decide to get a divorce not caring how it effects the children who suffer the most in divorces," said Brad.

"Yes, I agree. I remember when I lived in Oregon, there was a guy that would use his kids as an excuse for everything. I need off tomorrow could you work. Sorry, I am late I had to drive the kids to school because they missed the bus were just some of his excuses.

After using all these excuses one day he came into work asking off for the next day because he said his child was in the hospital. The manager saw through it and said, "No". Then the guy did not show up and he was fired. After him making up all those excuses, I would not blame the manager for firing him. I am so tired of lazy people that do this and expect the people that work to pay extra taxes to pay their bills while they live high on the hog," said Jake.

Meanwhile, Marc was driving to his daughter's house to check on her. As he walked in the house and he noticed she was doing the laundry. "Well I can see that you are starting to feel better now," he said. "My head still hurts a little bit but I think I will be ok," said Deseray. "I got some news about Paul's death some good and some bad," said Marc. "Well what is it," said Deseray? "There was a kidnapping the same night in the same alley so we think the murderer may be the same person. However, we found traces of medal that matches the piping in the alley in the blood that was smeared on the wall but we could not find the piping used to do the murder or fingerprints on the wall, the dumpster or on the piping," answered Marc. "I guess this means this person is pretty smart so I think I am going to go buy a handgun because the cops do a good job but cannot be everywhere at one time to defend you," said Deseray.

Back in the interview room Jake and Brad were having a hard time finding a new personal trainer. A woman named Sandy came in for an interview. She was about five foot four tanned with long blonde hair. Sandy decided to look for a job that was better paying then working at the tanning booth next door. However, Jake and Brad decided she was all looks, no brains trying to sell herself by her looks and was not buying any of her answers to their questions they asked. After they were done they told her goodbye and said they would call her if they needed her. Upon her leaving the room Jake, said to Brad "Yeah right, ok whose next," and they started to laugh.

Ten minutes later a beautiful dark haired woman from an island out in the Caribbean named Tatiana came in. She had just graduated from college with a degree in athletic training. When she sat down the first question was asked by Jake. That question was, "What did you do during your internship at Maizacopianna University?" "During my internship I was an athletic trainer at a soccer camp for poor kids in Mexico." "Sounds fun, was the job a paid internship or not," asked Brad? "It was free," answered Tatiana. "Well that is commendable. You got any questions for us," asked Jake? "This looks like a nice facility can I take a tour," she said. "Sure we have twenty minutes before the next interview. Brad and I will give you a tour," answered Jake. Then they took her on the tour.

Fifteen minutes later they walked up towards the front counter. Jake whispered to Brad, "Watch this." Then he walked up to Tatiana and said, "I would like you to meet some of our staff. This is Jane, Mindy, Cindy, and Jimmy." They all shook her hand and after Jane shook hers she gave Jake and evil stare. Then Jake with a smile winked towards Brad and they both escorted Tatiana out of the building. Once they walked Tatiana to her car she gave Brad her number. Jake told her, "This does not mean you are going to get the job." "I know but I can at least get something out of this. Like a man with a job so I do not have to work." Then all three of them laughed and she left.

When Jake and Brad walked back in the building Jane confronted Jake right away. "You are not going to hire her are you," she said. "I do not know we will see," said replied Jake. Then Jake and Brad walked into the interview room shut the door. Brad turned to Jake and said, "You are such a jerk." To which Jake replied with a smile, "I know it is so funny isn't it," and they both started laughing.

The next interviewee was named Kate. She had a Masters in Personal Training. She had ran a facility in a resort near the Great Lakes but wanted to move south below the Pennsylvania Turn Pike where they get less snow. The first question Jake asked was, "What measures did you and your employees take to cut costs in the facility?" Kate's answer was, "We bought more expensive machinery that could be used for multiple muscle groups and workouts that paid for themselves over time instead of individual equipment that only works one or two muscle groups. The individual ones cost more when you have to buy a bunch of them to do the same workouts and take up more space. Having to add on to the building would cost a ridicules amount of money as well. As for the individual employees I have them clean the windows inside and outside as well as clean the bathrooms instead of paying someone to do the work."

"That is impressive," said Brad. Jake went on with the next question. "What are some of the rules and techniques you use with people working out," asked Brad? "Well I try to put them on a diet of 57% carbohydrates, 30% fats, and 13% proteins. Now if that does not work I have a test to see if their metabolism needs say more fat, or protein to digest food faster. The preferred workout requires running nine miles a week and weight lifting four times a week. While weightlifting they will rotate from upper body workout on the first day to lower body workout on the second day. Then they will switch back to upper body on the third day and back to lower body on the fourth. After that they will repeat the process the next week, answered Kate. Jake replied, "Well, the interview is over and we still have one more candidate for the job to interview and if we call it will be tomorrow. Now I will escort you to the door."

The next candidate for the job was Tom Thomson. He worked in sports medicine and decided to move from western Pennsylvania. He was late to the interview and Brad asked him a couple of questions. Then they told him to leave and after he left they went to get lunch.

CHAPTER 6

Another Nice Night Out

After another sleepless night, Marc drove to the police station. On the way to the station he stopped at his favorite local diner. Marc walked into the diner and sat down at a booth. The waitress asked him what he would like to drink. He answered, "I would like a chocolate milk shake, please." Then he looked out the window across the street and down the same alley that Paul died in. "My daughter lost her mother, now she has lost her boyfriend. What in the world is going on," he thought to himself? When the waitress came back he ordered three pieces of French toast, some eggs, hash browns, and a biscuit with blueberry jam.

Just then another officer from the police force came in and started talking to him. "I have not been on the force long and I heard what happened to your daughter. One of the officers on the force told me you liked to eat here so I thought I would stop in to see if you were here and tell you, sorry about what happened to her boyfriend. If there is anything I can do to help just ask," he said. "There is nothing you can do but if I need help I will tell you," Marc replied. As soon as the officer was done saying that the waitress brought Marc his food and asked the other officer if he will be having anything to eat. The officer replied, "Just get me some coffee. I already ate." Then the waitress left to grab him some coffee.

After the waitress had left the officer turned to Marc and asked, "I heard it happened on a street close to this one but where exactly?" "In that alley," said Marc pointing out the window. The officer had no reply for that. Then the waitress brought the officer his coffee and poured Marc another cup of coffee. When they were done eating and drinking the officer paid for both his cup of coffee and Marc's food. Then they both drove to the police station. At the station Marc found out nothing to help them on his quest to find Paul's murderer or Mrs. Minkinson's husband. Then he drove to Deseray's house disappointed.

While Marc was driving to Deseray's house he thought about how his wife Sandra died. Deseray was only thirteen years of age and that weekend she spent at her friend Kristina's house while they were driving to the mountains in western Pennsylvania to spend time at their time share. On the way there they decided to take a detour and head to Gettysburg to see the town and the battlefield. After a red light turned green they started through the intersection. Then a pizza delivery boy ran the red light hitting Marc's car, flipping it over killing Sandra, dislocating Marc's arms, and bruising his ribcage. Marc still has nightmares about it till this day.

When he got to Deseray's house she greeted him with a smile. "I am glad to see you are feeling better," Marc said. "How is work," she answered? "Nothing new is going on at work, now that life is back to normal. What are you going to do with your life," Marc replied? I am still working on getting a concealed weapon carriers permit for protection," Deseray answered. "You know usually I would not approve of this but after Paul's death and Mr. Minkinson's kidnapping, I think it was a good idea to start working on that permit. On top of that, no one has a clue where the person or persons are," replied Marc. "What do you mean persons," asked Deseray? "Well what is the odds one person kidnaps someone and a couple hours latter kills someone else? Then that same person got rid of all the evidence that could have implicated him or her? Look I am not saying it is impossible but highly unlikely," Marc answered.

Deseray stood there for a second staring at her dad thinking about what he had just said. Then she said, "If this person is a serial killer it is possible but we will just have to see. We watched that whole series of movies about the psycho that eats his victims and he was pretty smart. In my mind a smart serial killer that is able do all that damage to people's lives and not get caught is not so far-fetched." "I hope this person or persons are not that smart. You know what let's just stop talking about it and go out to get a bit to eat," said Marc. Then they got in his car and left to eat in the city.

At 5:45 AM Kate walked into "Backbreakers." There Jake meet her at the door and showed her the procedures for the opening the facility. Then he gave her a tour of the place. After that he had Jane show her how to run the register. Jane also showed her the prices for club members and the prices for nonmembers. She also showed her the cleaning procedures.

When the day was over, Jake showed Kate the closing procedures and escorted her to the door. He opened the door then let her out after she walked away he heard Jane's voice say "Jake." After turning around Jane said, "I just want to say I am sorry about the way I acted last time I worked. I was sick and having a bad day." Yeah right, you were just jealous of that woman named Tatiana, he thought to himself. Then he said, "Brad and Tatiana are going to a local club tonight you want to go with me?" "Sure," Jane answered. "Pick you up at six and I will buy you dinner," Jake said. "Thank you," she said.

Finally, at 5:45 PM Jane stepped out of the shower and dried herself off with a towel. Then she went to her dresser pulling out black bra and panties. Then she put them on and went to the closet. In the closet she looked through all twenty dresses she had and picked out a red dress with a gold dragon in the middle. She started to put it on as she heard the bell ring. Oh crap! It is Jake, she thought to herself. Hurrying, she finished putting the dress on and walked to the door. She pressed the button on the intercom and said, "Jake is that you?" "Yes," he replied. "Come on up the door is unlocked my apartment number is 223. Go ahead and let yourself in."

Jake walked on up the stairs and opened the door to see no one in the living room. He then went and took a seat on the couch and Jane yelled from the bathroom, "I will be out in five minutes!" Jake answered, "Take your time."

Fifteen minutes later she walked out of the bathroom with her hair done up, bright red lipstick on, and a smile on her face. Then she saw that Jake had fallen asleep on the couch and that smile was straitened instantly. "Jake wake up," she said! Jake woke up to see Jane looking over him. He said, "You look stunning, Jane!" "Thank you," she replied!" "Let's go eat," said Jake and they walked straight out the door to his sports car.

On the way to the bistro Jane and Jake were going to eat at in the city Jane talked about when she was a child living fifteen minutes away from the city. She talked about swimming in the river nearby her house when she was younger and her Scottish Terrier she had as a child. Then Jake said, "Terriers, are they not the ones you see winning the dog shows a lot?" "Yes," she replied. "Huh," he said in reply.

Jake decided to change the conversation so he asked her if she drank. She answered, "Every once in a while." "This place we are eating at here has a decent selection of wines. You should try some with your food. I will show you which ones I like when we get there," said Jake. Finally, after five minutes more of listening to Jane talk about every little thing that came to her mind they arrived at the bistro.

Jake opened the door for Jane as they walked in and the host seated them at a table. Jane said, "Glass of water." Jake answered, "A bottle of Pinot Noir and two glasses." Jane started to look at the menu as the host went to get their drinks. Jake turned his head towards Jane and said, "You're definitely going to like this wine Jane." "Yeah, I am not much of a wine drinker but maybe you will turn me into one."

After looking at the menu for a little bit, the host came by with the drinks and said, "Your waiter will be with you shortly." Then Jane asked Jake, "How is the escargot?" "First-class," answered Jake. "What about the Calamari," she said next? "The same," Jake answered. Finally, the waiter came just as Jane was about to ask how the pasta and shrimp tastes.

"What will we be ordering today," asked the waiter? Jake said, "A Filet Minoan with a side of broccoli and potatoes. Then Jane asked, "The pasta with the shrimp or the pasta and linguine? Which one is the best?" "My favorite is the pasta with shrimp," the waiter answered. "I will have the pasta with shrimp with the salad bar and a side of green beans, as well as some corn," said Jane. The waiter left to go get their order and some bread for their table. Jane went to grab a salad and came back to see Jake having some bread to eat.

Jane tried the wine and told Jake that she liked it. Then she kept talking to Jake about everything that came to her mind. By the time they finished eating she had drank three glasses of wine and Jake was getting tired of her already. He thought, I hope she dances as well as she looks because all of her talking about everything that comes to her head is starting to annoy me. However, Jake was in for a pleasant surprise in the car on the way to the club. Jane fell asleep. This made him happy because now he knew if he ever wanted to get her to be quite he could just fill her full of alcohol and she would become drowsy and fall to sleep.

When they got to the club around ten o'clock Jake woke her up. They then walked in and grabbed a seat at a booth that Brad and Tatiana were at. Jake ordered some whisky with soda in it and Jane ordered some champagne. The whole group of them went dancing on the dance floor. Jane was a very good dancer she had spent many hours on the dance floor at clubs in college. She really lived it up in college where she joined a sorority. The reason she did this is she knew that where the sororities were the guys flocked too to get some action. Jane also wanted to take advantage of her light beautiful skin, young looking face, and her long black hair with five foot eight inch athletic frame, by playing the field in college.

In high school she tried to have relationships with guys but they all either cheated on her or left her because they were going off to college and they wanted to play the field as well. In college she forgot about all those guys after she saw how many good looking guys there was in college and decided to play the field as well. After college, Jane had enough of the high school and college mentality. She decided to settle down, maybe even have some children. This is what she planned to do with Jake but could she turn Jake away from his womanizing lifestyle? That was for time to tell.

At the club Jane and Jake were dancing as Kate walked into the club wearing a blue dress with high heels. She went to the bar and ordered a shot of hard liquor and slammed it down. Instantly guys flocked to her. Kate sat there a while letting the guys buy her drinks and talk to her, until she picked the best looking one and went to the dance floor. After a couple songs Jake and Kate ran into each other on the dance floor. Kate started dancing with Jake and Jane started dancing with Kate's dance partner. After the song was over they all went back to the booth including Kate. Then they started to talk with Tatiana and Brad, who were already sitting down talking to each other.

After some time went by they got a deck of cards and started playing a drinking game named links. Jane who was not good with alcohol after a couple of rounds started to loose badly and got very drunk. Then everyone at the table got back on the dance floor and started dancing. After a while Jake found himself dancing in between Jane and Kate. Jane wanted Jake badly so badly that she would deal with Kate's crap. Kate knew that Jane saw her as a threat with her long blond hair, her hour glass shape, and long well-built legs. Jane knew she was no match for Kate so she pulled the only move she knew that might be able to pull Jake away from Kate at least for the night. Kate said, I do not feel so hot," to Jake. Then she put her hand to her mouth pushed through the crowd and headed for the bathroom.

Jake saw her run to the bathroom and decided to go to the bar to sit down so he could wait for Jane. He knew she was in no condition to drive and he would have to take her home. The bar tender asked him what he wanted to drink. Then Kate sat down next to Jake lit up a cigarette and said, "Another shot of hard liquor. It looks like he is going to be driving someone home. He will be having water. "Jake laughed and Kate said to him, "Jane a lightweight?" "Yeah, it was a horrible first date. She is so self-absorbed. You should have heard her talking at dinner. I could not even get a word in," answered Jake. "Either your right or your just as self-absorbed and do not like giving the attention," said Kate. Jake began to laugh. Then Kate said, "Here is my number, take her back to her apartment. Then come back. When you get back call me I will be on the dance floor. Don't worry I will give you some attention." Right after Kate spoke those words, Jane walked out of the bathroom towards them and Jake asked her, "Are you ok?" "No, I think I need someone to drive me home," Jane replied. Jake replied, "Do not worry I will drive you home." While Jane was getting herself together to leave, Jake looked up at Kate. Smiling at each other they were both thinking the same thoughts. What a poor little girl. She is such a sap. Then Kate went back to the dance floor to steal her stud back away from some random women he was dancing with.

When Jane and Jake got back to Jane's apartment Jane ran to the bathroom and vomited in the toilet. Jake saw this and after she cleaned up, he helped her into bed. He told her goodbye and left to go back to the club. As soon as Jake left locking the door behind him, Jane started to cry. She knew as soon as she walked out of the bathroom and saw Jake talking on the phone that Kate was on the other side of the phone that she had no chance with him.

After Jake got back to the club he called Kate's phone and she did not answer. He went to the dance floor and did not see her there then he went back to the table. There he saw Brad and Tatiana sitting there. Then he sat down. "Oh there you are," and as Jake sat down Brad asked, "Where have you been?"

When Jake was just about to answer Kate slid into the booth beside him saying "Hi," and Jake answered Brad's question. "Taking Jane back to her apartment," said Jake. Brad shook his head and said, "As soon as we started playing links I knew she was in trouble." Everyone laughed then Brad said, "I think Tatiana and I are getting a little bit tired I think we are going to go home and get some sleep." Then Tatiana leaned her head on Brad's shoulder and said, "Your right Brad you always know what I want," in her sweet Hispanic accent. Then everyone started laughing harder. Finally, Brad said, "Goodbye," and Kate said, "Nice meeting you Tatiana."

After Brad and Tatiana left Jake turned to Kate and said, "You tired?" "No," Kate answered while grabbing him by the hand and leading him to the dance floor. They danced until closing time and they both went home to Jake's apartment.

CHAPTER 7

Sick Dark Individuals

PAST

In the back of an old abandon restaurant around 4:00 AM. Mr. Minkinson sat tied to a chair. He started to smell something and hear something boiling. One of the kidnappers asked him, "Remember my proposition I gave to you." "Yes," Mr. Minkinson answered. "What will it be then," asked the kidnapper. "No, I will never help you," Mr. Minkinson answered. "Well then, I was going to cook you some fried chicken to eat but I am going to cook something else," said the kidnapper. Having heard Mr. Minkinson's reply the kidnapper grabbed a cup and dipped it into the boiling grease. Then pulled the cup out unzipped the Mr. Minkison's pants and poured grease on his crotch.

Mr. Minkinson screamed in pain. Then the kidnapper said, "Am I getting the point through yet or do you need some more coaching towards the right decision. "I am good," answered Mr. Minkinson trying to hold back another scream. The kidnapper went out the backdoor of the old abandon restaurant, picking his phone out of his pocket. He dialed a number and said, "I just got a reply." "Good, I guess he saw it our way," said the voice on the other end. "Yes," said the kidnapper laughing.

Around 8:00 am on Saturday morning Jake woke up. Lying next to him in his bed was Kate. Kate leaned over and kissed him. "Thanks for the good night," said Kate. "Thank you! I hope you enjoyed it as much as I did," replied Jake. "I am going to cook breakfast for you. What would you like to eat," Jake asked? "Surprise me," she answered. "I will wake you up when I am finished," replied Jake.

Fifteen minutes later, Jake woke Kate up and brought a tray too her laying it on the bed next to her. She looked over to see two pancakes with some butter on the side, whip cream with strawberries on top. On the tray next to it was coffee with a sugar bowl and a chocolate milk shake. "Look's wonderful," Kate said. "I hope you enjoy it," replied Marc.

After she took a bite Kate said, "Wow, I had no idea you were a good cook." "Thanks, I did not know myself," Jake replied. "Oh you are so full of it," Kate said as she started laughing. They finished their meal and took a shower together.

While Kate and Jake were having fun, two men walk into a bank all masked dressed in black jumpsuits. One of them puts a gun to the bank tellers head. The other hopped over the counter to make sure no one touches any buttons or anything that might notify the police department which (if it happened) would result in someone getting shot. A third man walks in the bank and grabs a hold of the branch manager telling him to open the vault or he will be shot. He takes him in the back where no one can see him and has him open the vault. The branch manager tries to put the wrong numbers in and says, "I do not know the combination," "Yes you do but I do not need your help, so put the numbers I say into the key pad or I will shoot you," the bank robber said. "Ivan Minkinson is that you," said the branch manager. "Yes," now put the numbers I tell you in now," yelled the Ivan! The Ivan told him the numbers they opened up the door and walked in.

Once in the vault the Ivan had the branch manager unload the money into a bag. Then Ivan shot him right below the ribcage and left. As Ivan was leaving the vault room the other robbers had tied everyone else up except for one of the women tellers. One of the robbers put a gun that was in his coat pocket in her side and led her out towards the car. One of them said to the women, walk casually and do not cry just make it look normal or this gun that is in my pocket will go off. As they started to get into the car the teller asked them, "What do you want with me?" Your beautiful you figure it out," one of the robbers replied then pushed her into the car and speed away. They drove down to an abandoned auto shop a man rushed up to the car once they pulled it in the garage. With him, he had a new license tag to put on the getaway car. The women cried wondering what horrors she was about to go through. Then once they were well out of the city and into the country they drove down a long driveway into the woods down to a house with a pond next to it. One of them licked her on the face and said, "Get out of the car and strip down to your underwear." She did just as she was told and then he said, "Go jump in the pond and start swimming." She jumped in the pond as one of the robbers got out of the car. The robber grabbed her clothing got in the car and they all drove away.

One of the robbers started talking to the others. "Did you see the look on her face as she was crying? Man she was hot." "Yes, the look was the picturesque. You could tell she thought that we were all going to rape her especially after you licked her face. That was hilarious," one of the robbers said to the others. Then Ivan Minkinson said, "Shut up you sick freaks. I was only in this for the money. Why would you even consider raping a girl when you have all this money?

They all looked at each other for a second and shook their head in agreement. Then one of the criminals said, "Your right I just read a statistic saying that 63% of people said that they would consider cheating on their significant other for money. Just imagine how many more would do that if you say threw a couple hundred to thousands of dollars (which we all have now) into the picture so why would you need to rape a woman when you have all that money." Everyone else in the car looked at him for a second then started laughing at him.

After driving down the road farther the Ivan Minkinson pulled out his cell phone and called the other people that were involved in the bank heist. "Put me on the phone with Ivan Minkinson, he said. Then he pulled his mask off to reveal that he was not Ivan but just another robber. Ivan still tied up to a chair answered the phone. "Yes," he said in a weak voice. "Looks like you are in a world of hurt now," said the robber. "How is that," asked Minkinson? "Well you giving me the combination to the vault worked great even though we did not need it. We got tons of cash and everything worked out fine. However, since I am close to your height, sounding exactly like you and had a mask on. I said that I was you. Then I shoot your branch manager. You better hope he does not survive or you will be going to jail for a long time because he is the only one that heard me say that I was you," said the robber? Ivan started to cry then said, "Let me go! You got what you wanted! Just let me go!"

"Now come on do not be that way. You are too valuable to us now for us to let you go. You have a vast knowledge of the workings of the inside of a bank and bank systems just as you have told us. Oh, and one more thing. You are a liability now. If I let you go you will probably tell the authorities all the things you have seen and heard us do. Then they will search for us and come dangerously close to catching us but we always cover our tracks. They will not find us. On top of that, there is no way to get a positive identification of us if we leave no fingerprints, shoe markings, hair, or any other form of evidence. As I see it you might as well join us and make lots of money. No one is going to believe you but I will give you some time with my man Ray-Ray to help you make a clear decision, Mr. Minkinson." Then the robber hung up the cell phone and laughed.

"Mr. Minkinson turns to Ray-Ray and says, "What options do I have?" "Well you either you comply or we can talk it over. I could also turn you into the authorities. I am sure they will believe you," said Ray-Ray. "I will take my chances with the authorities and if they do not believe me, my wife will. They will at least work out a deal with me when they bring you guys in and I will not get a life sentence or death," replied Mr. Minkinson. Ray-Ray let out a laugh and said, "Wrong answer, close your eyes I got a surprise for you." Ivan kept looking at him as Ray-Ray put some safety glasses on Mr. Minkinson. Then looking over at a cup he picked it up and put yet another scoop of burning hot grease and through it in Mr. Minkinsons face. The grease was so hot it started burning through the safety glasses as Mr. Minkinson screamed.

Then Ray-Ray said, "For some reason I do not think your wife is going to want to spend all her time with you now. She might stick around but I do not think you will be the only one in her bed with her. If you do not feel the same I can just keep going till I have had my share of fun and end your misery." "Ok I will join you," Ivan said. "Good choice. At least now you will be able to afford plastic surgery and some girls will sleep with you just because you got money," said Ray-Ray.

Meanwhile, walking down the road shivering Maria was still trying to comprehend what had just happened. She was just glad the robbers did not rape or hurt her. However, it was getting dark and she needed to find a way to get warmed up before she got pneumonia. Maria finally got to the end of the long road that the abandoned house with the pond was on. She then started walking along the highway, trying to hitchhike her way back to civilization. The sun was down around the trees now. Maria thought the time was around 7:30 PM. Finally, after walking for five minutes along the main road a man in his early thirties pulled over and said, "Looks like you need a ride. Get in." Maria got in the car still shivering. "What happened," the man said. "Our bank got robbed and they kidnapped me," Maria answered. "Well they let you go. That is good isn't it," the man said as they drove down the main road back towards the city. "Yes it is but I am shivering. Do you have any clothes I can change into," she asked? Yes, in the suitcase in the back," the man said. Maria crawled in the back and changed into jeans with a t-shirt.

While Maria was changing she could not help but to look and see if the man was trying to get a glimpse of her in the rear view mirror. She wanted to see if he was staring at her to see if he was boyfriend material or if he was just a creep. He did not so when they got back into the town and to the police station she asked him wait for her so he could bring her home to her house after she was done telling the police what happened.

Maria got out of the car, told the man to wait there and walked into the police station to give them her statement. When she came out she asked the man to give her a ride home. As they were driving the Maria introduced herself to him and he told her his name which was Martin Benin. Maria told him thanks for his help and gave him her number. When they got to her house she kissed him goodbye and walked into her house to get some sleep.

The Monday morning Jake and Kate walked into Backbreakers together. Jane saw this and the smile fell from her face instantly. Then Kate turned to Jane with a smile on her face and said, "Good morning Jane, you look like you are doing better than you were Friday night. How are you today?" "Fine now that you are here. You brighten up my day because you're so funny," Jane replied. Brad who had just walked in maneuvered past everyone and into the men's locker room, covered his mouth and started laughing because what Jane had just said was full crap. "If we could just put them two in a cage match that would be worth watching," he thought to himself.

Backbreakers was a great place to be that day for Jake. Memberships were at an all-time high for the facility and Jake new he was staring a raise right in the face. He had his best friend Brad working with him and his woman Kate by his side. Life could not get any simpler for Jake.

Yes, finally that congealed alcoholic substance in Jake's body was beginning to turn into a heart. Kate had won his heart over. What he liked best about her was not just that she was a hot hard bodied blonde with nice legs but she was funny as well. However, everyone who worked at Backbreakers knew the real reason why they were perfect for each. A reason Jake could not see himself. This reason was Kate was just as cold hearted and soulless as Jake was. Yes, Kate was funny but she did not think about how what she says and does hurts others. Sometimes even Brad would get sick of her and would tell Jake how much of a prick she was being to people. He would also tell Jake that the two were not good for each other and that the whole thing seemed too good to be true. Brad also tried to explain to Jake that she was too much like him and that since he was a womanizer that she might treat men the same way as he treats women, like a piece of meat.

After Kate had worked at Backbreakers for a month she left Jake and her job. Kate did not just leave Jake she left him floored and with no reason why. The way she treated him was epic. Even Jake could not think of a more ridicules way to kick a person to the curb than she did. Kate's actions left Jake heartbroken and burned like a piece of meat left on a grill to long. It was as if Kate had ripped his heart out took a flamethrower to it and blew the ashes back in his face. Had Jake finally learned his lesson or was he simply to foolish to learn from the experience?

CHAPTER 8

Fun and Games

THE PAST

Jolene walked into the police station and up to Marc. "I am done my undercover work and in my opinion, Jake is too consumed with trying to get laid to think of a way to kill somebody," she said. "Good job Jolene. I was wondering if I could take you and my daughter out to eat. I am sure she would like to hear the details of what you and Jake did." "Oh definitely, that sounds like it would be fun," said Jolene!

Later that night, Jolene pulled her car into the parking lot of an upscale restaurant. She had on her rain coat over her nice darker purple (like the color of a glass of merlot wine) dress with flowers on the seams. Then she stepped out of her car in her open toed high heels to walk into the 1920's style restaurant. As she walked on the brick sidewalk, she tripped and almost fell to the ground. The only reason she did not fall is she grabbed hold of one of those gaint street lamps while purposely stubbing her big toe into the brick sidewalk to help hold her up.

Inside the restaurant Marc and Deseray were sitting at a table that was close a brick wall when Jolene walked in and Marc introduced her to Deseray. Jolene then sat down facing towards the Jazz band playing on the stage.

After that the waiter walked up and asked them what they wanted to drink. Marc ordered a soda, Deseray ordered some soda with a shot of hard liquor, and Jolene ordered a glass of Chardonnay. As the waiter left to go get their drinks Jolene excused herself to go to the bathroom.

In the bathroom Jolene examined her big toe to find out it was bleeding, the toe nail was cracked and starting to bruise. "I will never wear opened toed high heels again," she thought to herself. Then she walked out to join Marc and Deseray at their table.

When the waiter came back with their drinks, Marc ordered a sirloin steak, with a baked potato and broccoli. Deseray ordered a wrap that came with the salad bar and Jolene decided to get lasagna with bread sticks.

During dinner, Deseray asked, "What did you find out about Jake?" "Well, He is definitely not the killer. He is just another meat head to busy trying to get laid as well as too much of an ignorant, stupid, and vain idiot to be the killer. I also stayed at his place a couple of nights and I found no gun just a bunch of body building magazines and magazines of swimsuit models. On top of that, I was surprised to find nothing incriminating on his computer, other than porn, said Jolene."

"Guess this means Jake is just another loser with an alcohol problem who likes to womanize," said Deseray? "Yes normally, but not with me. His friend told me that he said I was the one and Jake has never said that before," answered Jolene. Both women laughed together. Then Jolene continued on by saying, "After what he did to you and your boyfriend. I decided to put him through the ringer. I told him my name was Kate. From the beginning I acted like I was all full of myself and got all my laughs at the expense of others. I even went as far as to steal him away from his girl. That poor girl is madly in love with him and I felt bad about stealing him but it had to be done so I could get the investigation over with.

"What was she like said," Marc? "Young, ditsy, naïve, and a very nice person, she probably hates me though after what I did to her. The jokes were mostly at her expense I probably gave her a complex if she did not already have one. I upstaged her on the dance floor at a club and after she got sick he was going to take her home but not before I gave him my number. Then I told him to come back to the club that night to hang with me and his friends while she was still in the bathroom. After he got back from dropping her off we danced awhile and went to his place. I feel really bad she probably cried herself to sleep and wished to die that night," replied Jolene. Then Jolene turned to the waiter and ordered some more hard liquor.

"How did you get rid of him," said Deseray. First, I started arguing with Jake over everything from, what restaurants to eat at, to what movies to watch then, and who should drive. Then I started flirting with other guys (that drove him crazy)," said Jolene. Then the waiter brought her the alcohol she ordered as Deseray started to laugh at what Jolene was saying.

"Next, I brought my cat over and it vomited on Jake's Afghan rug that cost him $500.00. When all of that did not work I acted like I was really drunk at a club one night and started dancing with another guy. I even grabbed his tight rear in front of Jake hoping to start a fight but the guy backed off when he saw Jake. Finally, we went home to his place and I got him really drunk. Once he was drunk I hand cuffed Jake to the bed naked. Then left him cuffed to the bed and pretended to go to the bathroom but I left out the window instead. When I got to my car I called his friend on his cell telling him his friend needed help. Then the other officers that were helping me investigate him did the rest. Jake called my number to find it was out of service and even went to the apartment that I was staying at for the whole operation only to find nothing, there not even furniture," said Jolene laughing.

Marc finally spoke up and told both them what he thought about what Jolene did. "Now look I agree Jake is a jerk but did you have to stoop down to his level Jolene? This is also nothing to laugh over Deseray? By doing what you did Jolene, which makes you no better than him in my mind. Maybe you should have backed off on Jake a little bit more and act like the mature one. Look you are twenty-nine years old almost thirty and a beautiful girl that is smart. Why don't you find a guy and settle down instead of playing super spy as well as wasting yourself on trash, drinking to death, as well as one night stands. You want to get married right?" "Yes, I do," she answered. "Look it is funny now but one day you will get tired of the games and want to settle down with a mature man maybe even have kids. However, how do you expect to ever keep a mature guy that wants to get married and/or have kids as well as stick around if he thinks you cannot take anything seriously either Jolene? After a moment of silence Deseray changed the subject and they continued to eat their dinner.

When the group was finished their meal and walked down the street to a local coffee shop. Then they talked about music, movies, and books for a while. Finally, after Jolene and Deseray exchanged numbers the group all went home.

PRESENT

Michael woke up to his morning ritual which was walking down the stairs and making a pot of coffee. Then he read the bible, when he was done he made breakfast for Karina and him. As he was cooking Karina woke up came down stairs in her robe and kissed him good morning. Then she walked outside to get the paper and sat down at the dining room table to read it.

When breakfast was done cooking he brought the food to the table. The food was eggs, bacon, and waffles with syrup, blueberries, butter, and whip cream. "This tastes great," said Karina. "What do you have planned today Karina," asked Michael? "I am going to the outlet stores and take a mile long walk looking through the stores then I am going to go swimming in that nasty canal to see if we can have two headed children from the pollution in there," said Karina. Then they both started laughing instantly knowing how polluted it once was.

"What are you going to do Michael," asked Karina? "I am going to write some then after lunch go to check on the restaurant," answered Michael. "Sounds exciting but I think I will act like a good stay at home house wife and spend some money on your credit card," Karina said as she started to laugh. Then she said, "Look, I will get the dishes you go have fun with the book." Michael got up from the table and walked up stairs with a cup of coffee in his hand to work on his book as Karina took care of the dishes.

After three hours of typing Michael got some lunch and went to wash up. After that he got in his car and headed to the restaurant on route 30. When he pulled into the parking lot, he parked the car, and pulled out his phone. Michael called his wife to tell her to be home at five because he had an important announcement to make to her. Karina told him she had some important news to. Then he walked into the restaurant.

As he walked into the restaurant the new manager walked up to him and said, "One of our customers has a complaint about one of the servers. This is the second time in two weeks. Should I fire him?" "That is your job to decide but if you want my opinion, yes. I do not do three strikes myself. I find if you screw up twice there is a good 80% chance it will happen again. Besides in an economy like this one we can get a better waiter anyway. Other than that how is the restaurant doing," said Michael. "We made a profit for the second month in a row," said the manager. "That is good. If you keep this up I will give you a raise. The last manager ran this place like his own little piggy bank and that started to irk me so that is why you are here and he is gone. Keep up the good job and get us ready for an inspection. We have not had one in a couple months. I think they will pop in here in the next couple weeks so you got a week and I will come check it out myself," Michael said.

After Michael walked in the grill area to check and see how the cooks were doing. Then the manager cracked a smile and thought, none of my employees better screw this up because if we get a lower score then the Chinese restaurant down the street that had a dog running through the back of the kitchen I am not going to be happy."

When lunch time rolled around, Michael told the cooks to prepare him a burger with barbecue and bacon on it. Then he headed to the mall. At the mall he got some ice cream, some cinnamon roasted almonds for Karina and bought some new running shoes, along with a nice pair of khakis. Finally, he headed to a travel agency picking up two tickets and headed home.

Karina was home with a London broil cooked on the table, some mashed potatoes, and carrots as well. They sat down, prayed, and started to eat. "You go first Karina. What do you have to say," asked Michael? "I am pregnant," said Karina! "That is wonderful let's celebrate," said Michael! Then he pulled out two tickets for a cruise to Brazil. Karina and Michael got up walking over to each other. Then they hugged. Karina said, "No actually, I only got a promotion at work at the bank. Just seeing the look on your face was what I wanted." "I hoped to enjoy another year of marriage first and do not worry. I will get you back for that one," Michael said as they were sitting back down to finish their dinner.

CHAPTER 9

"What's A Sand Test?"

The roar of the crowd echoed throughout the stadium as a locally favored soccer team scored the game win goal in Manaus, Brazil. Then the crowd started singing as the team celebrated their victory. As the singing and dancing was finishing up Karina and Michael started to leave the stadium.

"What a great game," said Michael as they walked out of the stadium. "Yes, it was way better than any of the professional soccer teams we would watch in America. These were only local teams and most of them played a lot better than the best American's can," replied Karina. Then they kissed each other just before they walked out of the stadium gates.

While Michael and Karina walked through the parking lot to the sports car they rented. They discussed the food they had at the stadium and where they were going to stay the night.

"The coffee was great and so was the coconut in the pudding that I had," Karina said. "My favorite was the Churrasco," said Michael. "What was that again," asked Katrina? That was the Brazilian barbecue, replied Michael. "That was good," said Katrina with a smile on her face as Michael and her stepped into the car to leave.

Karina and Michael talked about many topics in the car on the way to their next destination the restaurant. After they exited the car, walking to the restaurant Michael said, "Isn't it great all the fun activities they have to do in this country." Then he opened the door to the restaurant. "Yeah, they have so much pride in their country to and they are not as prejudiced as the people in America are. Yes, some of the political parties in America turn the races as well as the rich, poor, and middle class against each other to get votes. Then they have those people that treat soldiers like they are just a **"ALL"** a bunch of baby killers instead of understanding is the real baby killers are most the politicians who send everyone but usually their own sons and daughters off to war," replied Karina. "Yes the soldiers are just trying to survive, much less win the war, and the politicians who are supposed to be doing the same thing are using them as chest pieces in their own game or to make money," Michael said agreeing. "A couple of idiots do some war crimes and suddenly they are blaming all the whole army and the president for something they cannot control other than to throw them in jail," Karina replied.

"Dinner for two," said the hostess. "Yes," replied Michael. "It will be a ten minute wait," said the hostess. "That will be fine," answered Karina. Then they turned around and walked outside to wait.

"I cannot wait to go to Rio De Janeiro and to go shopping in Sao Paulo," said Karina. "Yeah, let's take a helicopter taxi when we go to Sao Paulo and go to Carnival, replied Paul. Then he paused for a second and said, "I hear it makes Mardi Gras look like a joke and the parade has all the different types of cultures of Brazil represented in it. Hopefully, they will have the Sumba and Cabrolara dancers in the parade." "What is Cabrolara," asked Karina? "It is Brazilian fighting concealed as a dance by the slaves when there used to be slavery here in Brazil. They made it to keep their owners from knowing they were readying themselves for a time when the slaves could revolt against them," answered Michael.

"Do not forget the rodeo and maybe we could see another soccer game," added Karina." "Another soccer game Karina. Was the game that good that you want to see another one," Michael said puzzled. "No, I just wanted to replace you with one of those nice tan soccer players or a country boy with a six pack," said Karina. "Well you go right ahead and when we get to Rio I will have to take one of these nice looking Brazilian girls for a sand test, get a divorce from you and leave you here so you can have your soccer boy or Brazilian cowboy, but it will not last long because you will be broke," Michael said laughing.

"Now do you think I would cheat on you, Michael," asked Karina? "No, Well, maybe if he had a lot of money and was trampled or gored by one of those bulls he might get enough pity points for you to leave me," replied Michael. "You are so full of it," said Karina as they started kissing. "The weather is great here. I cannot wait to see, you in your new bathing suit," said Michael as they continued to kiss. Then Karina asked "What is a sand test?" "I will tell you later," said Michael. Suddenly, Karina turned away from the kiss and said, "No, you are going to tell me now or you are not going to see me in my new bathing suit. Instead, I am going to wear cutoff jeans and a tee shirt, so you cannot get the satisfaction of the fact that all those men will be staring at me in my bathing suit wanting me but unable to have me," Karina said smiling. "Yep, yeah whatever, they will be staring at you anyway," replied Michael. "You're right, I am that hot, and nice save," Karina said in reply as she started kissing Michael again.

Five minutes later the hostess returned to take them to their table. "What a great place Brazil is," said Karina. "Of course where else can a shoe boy can become president," replied Michael, as they walked to the table?"

When they reached the table the waitress asked what drinks they would like. Then she told them the special of the day. After that she left them alone to look at the menu to decide what they wanted to eat and took their drink order to the bar to tell the bar tender their order.

When the waitress had left the table Michael and Karina started to look at the menu. "Look at all this wonderful food," Karina stated. After a slight pause she added look at this one. It is called pato no tipuci. The main ingredients are duck, garlic, and jambu," stated Karina. "Sounds delicious, let's order it," replied Michael.

A couple minutes later the waitress returned with Michaels shot of hard liquor, as well as Karina's glass of red wine. Then they ordered their meal and continued talking about everything from music, to sports, business, religion, and politics, until their meal was over. After that they tipped the waitress 30 % then bought a bottle of champagne to take back to the hotel and left.

By the time they showed up at the hotel Karina had developed a headache from the red wine and was no longer feeling so well. However, Michael and Karina both knew what to do, open up the bottle of champagne, and have a couple of drinks while the chemical in the wine wore off. Then they went to the balcony of their hotel room sat down and open up the bottle of champagne and had a couple of drinks.

After about two drinks Karina's head began to numb and she could not feel the pain no more. Karina turned on some Sumba music and they began to dance till two in the morning. When they were finished dancing they both decide to go to sleep. Michael told her that he loved her and they kissed each other goodnight and feel asleep.

In the mourning Michael and Karina woke up and got breakfast ordered into their hotel room. Then they got dress. While they were getting dressed Karina said, "I cannot wait till we get to get to Sao Paulo tonight and take a helicopter taxi over the city while we enjoy dinner together." "Well I got a surprise for you Karina. Guess where the helicopter ride is going to end?" "Where," she replied? "We are going to a stadium, to watch a techno concert. I found out your favorite Euro style techno band was playing in Sao Paulo when I was searching the internet for a good place to go on vacation and while I was checking out activities to do in Sao Paulo I saw a their concert was tonight," answered Michael. "Wow, you would be the best husband ever except for one problem," said Karina. "Gee what could that be Karina the sand test," said Michael? "Ho-hum," replied Karina. "Do not worry you will learn soon enough," answered Michael.

After breakfast they got a helicopter ride to Sao Paulo. When they finally landed they left the high rise building to go shopping through the traffic jammed streets. "Now I know why the businesses here take employees places in helicopter taxis these streets are so busy," said Michael as they walked past local venders."

Later on, after the married couple got down to the streets Karina said, "Look, there is a humongous fish on that table." The vender told them in Portuguese that the fish was from the Amazon and how much it was worth and they turned the fish down.

Karina and Michael walked farther to see another table full of jewelry and behind the table hung up in the tent was some swim suits and surf gear. Karina picked up a surf board for when she and Michael would hit the beaches. Then they went into a local restaurant for food.

Meanwhile, Jake and Brad walked through the airport in Chicago. They saw a sax player playing nearby the compact disc store in the airport. Jake stopped and threw a tip inside his saxophone case. Then they walked into the music store. While inside Brad and Jake both bought jazz albums for the flight. Then they walked out and hit the bar at the airport and Brad started an interesting conversation with Jake.

"Why don't you come to church with me Jake," asked Brad? "What brought this up," asked Brad in reply? "Oh I do not know. "Maybe, in my opinion what you did to Jane was not to cool," said Brad. "Yeah, I feel bad about it still till this day she still will not open up to me about it. She looks a little disappointed," replied Jake as he took a drink of beer. "A little," Brad laughed. "Ok!!! A lot, I do not know whether or not she will forgive me," said Jake. You know that does not matter. If she cannot Jesus can forgive you," said Brad. "Oh really, look what happened to every one of his followers except for John," replied Jake. "Well yeah, that did happen but what about Paul? He walked around with warrants and nodding at the condemning of a bunch of Christians and Christ spared him after he knocked him off his horse. Paul went on to save tons of people and write a quarter of the new testament, so if he can forgive Paul I think she can forgive something so little like what you did," replied Brad. "Ok, but if they try to shove their religion down my throat I am out. Do you understand," said Jake?

Just then Tatiana walked into the bar. "Glad to see you guys made it to Chicago. Ready for Brazil," she said? "Yes, so how was meeting with your friends," said Brad. "Great!" she replied. "Well I hate to cut this short but it is time to get to go board our plane," said Jake.

Back in Brazil, night time is setting in while Karina and Michael are on another helicopter eating dinner. "This prime rib is delicious, tender and juicy," said Karina. "Yes, it is and so is the Champagne to," Michael said agreeing. Then the female helicopter pilot which was giving the tour interrupted by saying, "The meat is from Brazil, which is one of the top selling cattle producing countries in the world." Michael interrupted by asking, "I heard there are very few females in your profession. How did you get the job?" "Well memorizing all these coordinates and locations on these maps is one of the major hurdles before taking the test," the pilot stated. "The streets of Sao Paulo are so crowded but is it really worth all the money spent on gas to have helicopter taxis running everywhere," asked Karina? "Well the businesses think so and they control the money," replied the pilot.

After Michael and Karina had finished eating they sat there enjoying the rest of the scenery on the tour. Then Karina fell asleep content in Michael's arms which ended fifteen minutes later with the pilot interrupting Karina's sleep. "We have reached our destination I hope you enjoyed your flight. Have a nice evening enjoy your concert and come fly with us again," said the pilot. Then the helicopter landed on the helipad on the roof of a mall and a man dress in a tux walked to meet them half way from the door of the rooftop.

"Mr. and Mrs. Essential I presume," said loudly by the man in the tux. "Yes," Michael called back. "Follow me," said the man as they walked into the building and into an elevator. They took the elevator to the lobby. Walked outside and entered the limo that was waiting for them. The driver asked them where to go and the Essentials replied, "The area where the concert was at," and they left.

While the Essentials were having fun at the concert a woman was stuck in a warehouse tied up to a chair watching a man get tortured. "How could you have done this? You screwed up the sale," said the mysterious man as he turned to the man that was tied up in the chair next to her telling him, "Do not worry though we will fix this problem so that this never happens again." Then he pulls a saw he had sitting with the blade in the fire out and began the castration of the man in the chair.

After their flight to Brazil was over Brad, Tatiana, and Jake left in a luxury car to their hotel in Rio De Janeiro. Then they ordered dinner and Jake started to get drunk. Followed by Jake playing some card games at a local casino, while Brad and Tatiana spent time together back at the hotel room. By the time the night was over Jake had won sixty thousand dollars and the attention of a nice tan and voluptuous Brazilian women who was a model. Finally, the night ended with the model and Jake off the coast of Brazil on a Yacht Jake had rented.

In the morning after the concert Karina and Michael had breakfast in the hotel restaurant in Sao Paulo. They shared an orange salad and had some tea, corn cake and bananas. After that they walked to a local coffee shop and bought some Brazilian made coffee. Finally, they packed their bags and took a helicopter taxi to a place to rent a car to drive to Rio De Janerio.

Later on, when the jeep pulled up to the hotel that was on the beach front, Karina woke up with a smile. Then Michael said, "Looks like you missed the best part of the drive the Brazilian countryside. Maybe we should not have stayed up so late last night." "Why do you care? You got laid last night. The concert was amazing and so were you," Karina said with a smile. "Thanks for the ego lift honey," Michael replied. Then they kissed.

After the Essentials checked into the hotel they changed their clothing. While Karina was still changing, Michael headed out to the beach ahead of her to enjoy the waves. By the time Karina had come out to the beach and put the beach towels down Michael had come back from body surfing the waves to where Karina was laying down and she stood up to meet him. Just then Michael realized she was wearing the shirt and jeans they had talked about in Manaus after the soccer game. "I did not think you were serious about finding out what the sand test was. All you had to do was ask me and I would have told you what a sand test was. You think I would have you run around in jeans all day," said Michael? "Well, what is it," said Karina in a stern voice. As Michael began to open his mouth to answer her two men on all-terrain vehicles picked Karina up and drove down the beach with her. Then Michael gave chase but could not keep up and called the police.

That night on a huge yacht Karina woke up tide up to a chair gagged to see another women tide to a chair and gagged as well. It was the women from the warehouse. Five minutes later their abductors walked in and the man in charge (the same man who performed the castration) walked in telling the others to leave him alone with the two women.

As the two men left the castrator turned to Karina and said, "I guess you would like to know what you are doing here. Well we intend to sell you into a prostitution ring, so do not act up or you will end up like this." The man grabbed the back of the chair the women from the warehouse was in and dragged her away from Karina towards the corner of the room. Then he walked out the room. A minute later he returned with a blow torch and melted the women in the corners face off as Karina tried to scream but could not because of the gag in her mouth. Then the man left the room with Karina staring straight into what used to be the face of a beautiful woman's limp dead body.

Two hours later the crazy man who burnt the woman's face off returned and pulled the gag out of Karina's mouth and says, "You promise to be good and I will untie you." Karina agreed and he untied her and took her outside on the deck. There they start to eat dinner with a man form Argentina that wanted to buy her to be his wife.

While the buyer, seller, and the victim ate dinner. They discuss what price to buy Karina for, Karina looks around noticing there are two guards with two automatic assault weapons. One was an assault rifle that could be switched from semi to automatic. The other was a normal military grade machine gun. Then she started to think that this was a small ship and that there could not be too many people on board. There might be just the ship's captain, a mechanic, and a couple more guards on the boat. From that point on she decided to take the boat over but for now she would go along with the program and act like she wanted to be sold just to get away from the psycho that burned that poor woman's face off. Karina also had a plan and decided to wait till the opportune time to execute it.

Darkness started to fall as the meal went on and everyone started to get drunk off the wine and champagne. Karina actually drank some because she knew she had a high tolerance for drinking in college when she would out drink all the girls and even some of the guys in the swim house. Now they were all drunk and she thought it was time to put her plan into action.

First, Karina decided to take out her new Argentina husband who just bought her for $25,000.00. I am going to make this guy pay she thought because I am only worth the price of a piece of junk, gas guzzling, American made pickup truck. I do Japanese cars not government owned piece of junk. Not only am I a slave to him now I am worth close to nothing. He will pay for that she thought.

"I was wondering if we could get some candlelight for dancing a samba to celebrate my new Argentinean husband," said Karina. The seller agreed as long as he could light the candles and he went to get a lighter. Since, he did not have one he brought up the blow torch he used to melt the girls face off, he then lit the match and took the torch down to the bottom of the first steps to the stairs to the first level below the deck and came back up the stairs. By the time he returned Karina and her new husband was dancing to Samba music.

Towards the end of the song Karina started kissing the Argentinean man and the Argentinean asked to be left alone with her. The man who abducted her reluctantly agreed and left the two alone but had the guards watch from a distance. They danced one more song then Karina laid on the table they were eating on and told the man to come to her. Then she wrapped her legs around him tight while she was kissing him. Then he started to take his shirt off and as he was doing so Karina laid down on the table grabbed a steak knife. Jumped up grabbed him by the throat while he still had the shirt over his head and slight his throat.

After that Karina threw him overboard and she ran down stairs to get the blow torch but before she could make it down the stairs the guards started shooting at her from behind and another one from down the stairs was shooting at her as well. Then she threw the knife at him hitting him in the arm causing him to miss and hit the guard behind her. Out of an act of desperation she dived off the stairs onto the guard in front of her knocking him down and pulled the knife out of his arm and stabbing him in both of his eyes. The screams sent everyone scrambling to get her before she could kill everyone else. As she ran through the lower parts of the boat, (now with the guard's machine gun and a knife) she started killing everyone one by one trying to find the engine room.

However, when Karina got to the engine room it was heavily guarded by men with military grade assault rifles and machine guns so she turned around and decided to fight her way back up the stairs but she was surrounded and she decided to back into a storage room. In the storage room she finds several oxygen tanks, acetylene tanks for welding, ropes, and floatation devices. Karina quickly ties several floatation devices to two oxygen tanks and acetylene tanks. Then she put the oxygen tanks on and taking the ropes that had the acetylene tanks tied to them she draped them over her shoulders so she could carry them.

Just then the door was kicked open and the fighting continued. Karina took them all out one by one while making her way to the stairs. Running out of ammo Karina picked and assault rifle up off of one of her attacker's dead bodies and started blowing nice size holes into her adversaries.

Once Karina made it to the stairs she emerged slowly wondering what's next and noticed there was no one up the stairs that she could see, even though she knew they were up there just hiding so she had a go at it and walked up the stairs. Almost immediately four guards appeared with their weapons pointed at her. Then the man that tried to sell her pulled the assault rifle away from her spun her around towards him and said, "Where do you think you are going?" "Nowhere and neither are you," Karina replied. Then she stabbed him in the midsection with the knife she got from the table they were eating at and spun him around her to use him as a human shield. Then she backed to the side of the boat as the guards tried to shoot through him to get to her.

After that she dived into the water and dragged the floatation devices, oxygen tanks, as well as acetylene tanks behind her while swimming over to a Jets Ski tied to the yacht. Then under fire now from the guards she turned on the Jet Ski and speed away. Another guard got on another Jet Ski to go after her while yet another guard started lowering a speed boat off the yacht to chase after her.

However, the guard on the Jet Ski chased Karina shooting at her. Then when he was close enough she let off the gas and as he passed by her she threw an acetylene tank at his head knocking him out so she could then take his assault rifle. Once, she had the assault rifle she headed back towards the yacht. On the way back to the yacht the guards noticed she was coming back and started firing at her. This changed Karina's mind about taking the ship and she decided to tie one of the O_2 tanks to hold the accelerator in place. While she kept the rest of the tanks in the seat aiming the Jet Ski in the direction of the ships engine room and jumped into the water with a floatation device and the assault rifle.

When Karina popped up out of the water she had a smile on her face. However, that smile would soon change to a look of horror when the Jet Ski hit the yacht and the yacht exploded sending shrapnel everywhere. The shrapnel included an acetylene tank that had spewed out all the acetylene because a bullet hit it earlier. Karina tried to avoid the acetylene but it came at her head to fast for her to duck down into the water to avoid being knocked out.

Five minute later, Karina woke up lying on top of a piece of the yacht that was large enough for her body to lie on top of. Blood was leaking from her fore head as everything she was seeing started to come into focus. The first sight she saw was one of the guards holding on to the piece of the yacht. Then she looked at the water around her. Dead bodies were floating everywhere and the waters color was now red with blood.

"Help me up onto the debris please," said the guard. "Why should I help you," replied Karina? "I pulled you up onto this piece of debris," the guard answered as blood flowed from his back. "Well, you ruined my vacation and possible my life and…," said Karina with a sudden pause because before Karina could finish the rest of what she was going to say she noticed fins circling around the dead bodies, the guard, and her.

"Well, I might die but not right now, because you are going to save my life," Karina said while smiling. "What are you talking about

I already did," the guard said. "No, you did not. Not yet, but you're going to." Then she kicked the guard in the head as hard as she could knocking him off the piece of yacht and grabbing on to the piece of debris she swam as hard as she could away from him until she got away from all the blood that was in the water.

After that Karina stopped swimming and threw herself back onto the piece of the yacht. Turning back around she saw that the dead bodies were being pulled under the water by the sharks and the guard was gone. She then ripped off a piece of her shirt to use to try to stop the blood from bleeding from her forehead poured some seawater all over the piece of debris she was on to get the blood off of it. Finally, exhausted she leaned back against the piece of debris tired and passed out yet again.

Twenty minutes later, Karina woke up to two people pulling her out of the water. When they pulled her up on the deck of the yacht her sight came into focus to see that it was Jake and the Brazilian women that had picked her up out of the water. "Looks like she has a nasty cut on her forehead, thank God I used to be surgeon before I became a model. Get a bottle of alcohol and my first aid kit we are going to have to sew this up immediately," stated the Brazilian women!

While, the Brazilian women sewed up Karina's forehead Jake drove the yacht back to shore and asked how Karina got into the situation she was in. Karina told her story. Then thanked the Brazilian women and Jake for what they did.

When Karina, Jake, and the Brazilian reached shore they took Karina to the hospital. After Karina was checked out of the hospital they took her to the police station to fill out a report on the kidnapping. Soon after the police had taken down her statement, Jake drove her to the hotel and left.

Karina could not find Michael anywhere so thinking he was looking for her she went out to the beach. When she walked onto the beach she did not see Michael so having had plenty of sleep on the boat and in the hospital Karina decided to get some exercise by swimming.

After Karina had hit the water as Michael walked up on the beach and sat down not close enough to see that Karina was swimming in the water. Exhausted from looking for Karina all day he decided to sit and watch the sunset. Then as he looked up at the sun as Karina emerged from the water in her bathing suit touching her head around the stitches because her head was hurting due to the fact she forgot to not get the stitches and wound wet so soon.

Michael started to run towards her. When Karina saw him her reaction was quite different. She stood there with a stern face waiting for him to put his arms around her but as he went to grab hold of her she moved out of the way and pushed him from behind into the water laughing at him. Michael picked himself out of the water realizing it was a joke and started laughing to. Then they started kissing each other. As they kissed Karina asked, "Well, what is a sand test?" Michael answered, "The guys in Rio take the women to the beach for the first date to see if the woman is worth being in a relationship with."

Immediately after Michael answered her Karina pushed Michael into the water again saying, "That is so lame. I cannot believe I almost died floating on a piece of debris with one of my last thoughts being. What is a sand test? Just think I would have gone to heaven and asked that as one of my first questions. God would have answered me and everyone in heaven including God himself would have laughed at me after he answered the question because of how stupid that question was. That would have been pretty embarrassing. Just for that we are not having sex tonight as your punishment." Michael grabbed her and pulled her into the water with him saying, "Yeah right." Then they started laughing and kissing right there in the water.

CHAPTER 10

Misdeeds, Idiots, & Partying

"That is how I survived the kidnappers. Jake helped me do it, I told you," said Karina to Deseray as they sat outside a restaurant eating soft-shell crabs from Maryland. "I do not believe it," replied Deseray (who was sitting next to Kate)! After a quick pause Deseray said, "If he would have never started that fight we may have never run into Paul's killer and my life would have been better. I will never forgive him," Deseray finished! "Look I know you are upset Deseray but that is the truth I am telling you. Jake saved my life and I thank him for it." "No, He is not that great of a person. He just saved you because you are his friend's wife. That's all if you were just any old regular person he would have left you there to die and went off in that yacht, screwing around with that Brazilian model. Get real," answered Deseray!

"Ok then next topic," Karina said with force. How about those soft-shell crabs? Did you like them," asked Karina? "Yes, they were delicious," replied Deseray with a smile on her face, relieved to get away from the subject altogether." "So find any other guys other than Jake," said Karina laughing? "Yeah," said Deseray staring at Karina with a look of disgusted. "Well, what does he do for a living," asked Karina. "He is a seaman," said Deseray. "Oh that's going to last," said Karina sarcastically. "No, I was just kidding he is a shoe salesman," Deseray said with a smirk on face.

"Well then what is his name and what is so good about him," as Karina pushed for more information? "He does not do all the crazy stuff Paul used to do like repelling off cliffs and having a helicopter airdropping him into a wave that could kill him to surf. I do not think I could deal with someone else dying out of nowhere in my life and his name is Jared. Jared can cook excellent; cleans house and himself well. He also treats me nice and gives me lots of ice.

"Wait! You forgot to add two minor details. 1. Jared likes to and picks out his own drapes because he is gay. 2. You must like S & M because he spends all his money on you and is whipped. Where did you find this lost, poor, loser? Do not tell me you like him. He sounds pretty boring and not the least interesting at all. Tell me he is at least good looking," said Karina.

"Well, he looks good when he dresses up," Deseray answered. "That is weak sauce and completely lame. I am going to fix this by taking you out on the town later tonight," replied Karina. Karina looked up at the waiter and summoned him to the table asking for the check. Then she pulled out her cell phone called her husband and said she was taking Deseray out tonight. Then she called some of her girlfriends up asking if they would like to come.

When the women left the restaurant it was dark out so they passed an alley not noticing two men assaulting another man deep in the alley. "Pay up whack job. This is what you get for trying to steal from us," the one thug said to the man while punching the man in the mouth hard sending blood squirting into the air. Then the other thug threw the man on the ground and kicked the man in the rib cage till the bones cut strait up into his lungs causing him to vomit up blood. "Well where's the money," the man said still kicking him.

After a brief pause in the brutal beating one of the thugs pulled out a knife. The victim of the beating got on his knees and started to plead with the thugs, "Please give me more time I will get it," he said crying with blood covering his face and shirt from him coughing up the blood." With a look of disbelief and disgust on his face, the man with the knife said, "Do you have kids?" "Yes!" the victim said, hysterically. "Well when they see your dead body this will be a lesson to them on why hard work is better than stealing. Oh and by the way we are going to leave a little note showing your kids how much of a loser their dad really was." Then the thug slit the man's throat leaving the knife in the wound.

While the guy's body was still twitching on the ground the thugs discussed how they would write the note and get rid of the rest of the evidence. "Write a letter! What did you bring a typewriter, a computer, or some crap," said the one thug to the other sarcastically? "Oh, come on you think I am stupid or something? Who uses a typewriter? Look we are going to use a pen. What did you think I typed a letter or something? Did you know certain printer companies can tell what printer a letter was printed on," said the lead thug. "No," said the other thug. "Well that's why I was put in charge of this operation because I make sure I cover all the angles. If you were in charge we would have got caught doing crimes like this and you would have been bubba's little girlfriend not me," said the lead thug.

"Not after I put you in a wheel chair on our first day in jail. Then Bubba would have preyed on you because you are the weakest link and you could not have gotten away, being in a wheel chair and all," replied the other thug. "Come on dude. Do not take things so seriously. I am just showing some fearless gamesmanship, confidence, and charisma. All of which you lack. That is why you are always the wingman and I get the girl," said the lead thug. "Ok that's it. You're not even going to make it to jail. I am putting you in a wheelchair now," replied the other thug. "You are forgetting the task at hand. We have to get rid of the murder weapon. Then you can concentrate on putting me in the wheel chair later. I will write the letter while, you get the knife out of him and start to clean up this mess. I want to make sure this guy's kids know what a real jerk this man, no child was," replied the lead thug.

HOURS LATER

"Where are we going to hide the murder weapon," said the one thug, on company grounds, on Mr. Indifference's property, or the usual?" "The usual," replied the leader of the two thugs while driving the car over the New York state border.

When they got to the harbor they went to the end of a fishing pier and threw the knife in the water. Then they went to their hiding spot and burned their clothing they had on when conducting the murder.

Early in the morning, Marc was standing at the crime scene reading the letter that the two criminals wrote while the police car lights flash all around him. It stated:

> Dear, Detective in charge,
>
> This is what happens when you mess with us. We do not only kill you we expose all your skeletons of you and your family. Yes, not only did this man steal from us. This man cheated on his wife with strippers at a local club, especially with Miss Shoe Shiner. If you think I am kidding check out the local strip club. He stole hundreds of thousands in local taxes from the city and was involved in a drug smuggling ring. Oh and I forgot to mention a money laundering scam as well. What a standup guy! The best of society!
>
> P.S. Be sure to tell this man's family. Maybe his kids will not grow up to be a little turd causing problems for people like their daddy. Nothing hurts more than the truth.
>
> Cheers!
> Ace and Dice

"You know even though these guys are going to jail. They are right about two key points in this letter," said Marc to the police officer next to him. "What is that sir," replied the Officer Brennonhan. "Well I meet the guy once and he was supposed to help me go through some city financial records when investigating some funny business that one of the local politicians was involved in and he did not cooperate to well. Now we know why and this guy really irks me. I cannot wait to see the look on his kids and wife's face when they find out about this, especially his wife, who married a complete jerk. Tell me who does that," asked Marc? "I do not know but I would like to see the look on the wife's face as she punches that little stripper in the face. Oh what was the other point they were right about," the Officer Brennohan said posing another question? "Nothing hurts more than the truth. Too bad the wife will probably not tell the kids and they will still grow up to be just as morally corrupt as dad," said Marc. "That is sad to think about," said the officer.

After a slight pause Marc said, "Officer Brennonhan." "Yes sir," he replied. "Get on the phone to dispatch. Tell them to get some local officers to meet you at the local strip club tonight. You know the rest," said Marc. Then Marc went to his jeep as Officer Jamal Brennonhan walked over to his convertible sports car to leave.

Later, that night Deseray and Karina entered a club and walked to their normal table near the dance floor. When they got there Jolene, Karina, and Tatiana were sitting at the table. The girls ordered their drinks and sat down talking. "Where's your husband Michael," said Jolene? "What s up with you and married men you are obsessed because you talk about them or ask all the time," replied Deseray? "She just wants something she can never have," Karina said with a laugh. "Come on," said Jolene, "I will settle down but I am going to enjoy life while I am young. Married men love me because I am not a nagging bore like most their wives are. I bet you wish you had a little more fun before you got married?"

"One reason you are married men's favorite is because they know that you will give out, being used for sex, and he can home to his wife. Another reason is that they can just leave you because you do not require any commitment or responsibility so basically you are just a toy on the side they can dispose of. On top of that, it must be especially fun if you blacked out and woke up next to some guy, (you do not even know his name) only to find out you missed your period and are pregnant with his kid a month later," said Karina.

"Oh, wait a second; I forgot here is an even better one. Try waiting till you are forty to get married like some people do. Most those people end up with a six or a seven they do not even like because the 8's, 9's, and 10's do not want to marry a 40 year old. However, if you want to be picky go ahead and end up marrying someone you do not like because you'll become scared of dying alone. What a waste," stated Karina!

The table went silent for a moment and Jolene for the first time in her life, (even though she was hurt by the comment) had no sharp come back to say. Then Tatiana sensing an awkward moment replied, "Way to be a joy kill Karina. How about we head to the dance floor?"

When they got to the dance floor Karina, Kate, Deseray, and Tatiana started dancing together. Meanwhile, Jolene grabbed the attention of the first attractive man she saw and started dancing with him. After the song ended Kate, Karina, and Tatiana walked back towards their table to see Michael, Brad, and Jake waiting there. Tatiana said, "Hi Brad" and sat down next to him. Karina saw Brad there and turned to Michael, picked up her purse and said, "Hi, Michael it is a surprise seeing you here. I thought I would try a different club tonight. How are you?" "I am fine thought the same thing," he replied. "Well, I am going to freshen up," said Karina. Then she started heading towards the bathroom.

About halfway towards the bathroom (out of sight of the view of the table) Karina redirected herself towards Jolene. She grabbed Jolene by the arm and said, "Follow me."

Both women left the dance floor. Heading in the direction of the bathroom leaving the man Jolene was dancing with utterly confused. The man's situation change as soon as Deseray, (who was dancing with her back turned toward Jolene) turned around to see Jolene gone and a handsome man there so she started to dance towards him.

After entering the bathroom door Jolene asked Karina, "What is this all about?" "Jake is out there," answered Karina! "Oh no, How did he know I was here. I thought it was girl's night out," replied Jolene. "I thought so too," answered Karina. "Well I have to get out of here. Jake cannot see me here otherwise he will ask questions," said Jolene. "Don't worry I can fix this problem," said Karina. Then she grabbed her phone and did a three way call between Kate, Deseray, and her. "Guess who is here," said Kate. "Who," they both said?" "Jake," Karina answered!

"Ok here is what we are going to do. Kate you dance with Jake even though you do not want him anymore. I will help sneak Deseray and Jolene out. Kate wait till the next song to dance with Jake so it does not sound suspect," said Karina.

Right after the song ended Kate asked Jake to dance. Then Deseray grabbed the man she was dancing with by the tie and asked him to go somewhere private. After that Jolene, Deseray, and the man left out the back door. Jolene went home and Deseray took the handsome man to a bar.

During breakfast the next morning Karina asked Michael what the men were doing at the club that night. Michael answered, "I knew that Jake and Jolene could not be seen in the same club together so I did not go to the regular place, thinking that your group of women would not be there." "Well why didn't you at least call me and tell me you were going out? Did you not at least think what would have happened if they were in the same bar together and what about Deseray? Did you not think that she would want to be away from Jake after what happened to Paul? She still thinks Jake killed him you know," asked Karina? "Yes that would have been hilarious. Just imaging the argument and the words that would have been said between the two, we could have filmed it and put it in a movie or on the internet. It would have been so entertaining," replied Michael. "Shut up you jerk," Karina replied laughing.

Then Karina got real serious and said, "Michael look at me in the eyes and tell me you will call me next time. God Jane even had to dance with Jake and she is still pissed at him!" Michael looked into her eyes and said, "Do not worry I will call you next time," but before he could get the words next time out of his mouth he started laughing though.

Karina's face got real red. "Why did I marry you? Can you ever be serious? Wait do not answer that question," she said as she walked toward their bedroom, shutting the door behind her? Oh crap, Michael thought as he walked to the door to say he was sorry.

When Michael got to the door he realized it was locked. He said that he was sorry and Karina answered, "No, you are not, your just saying that. No, wonder sixty percent of marriages are ended by the women. Guys never change." "Well Hun, I do not remember the wedding vows saying anything about anything anybody changing. I did hear him say something about sickness and health, rich or poor? Do you remember that? If you were not happy with the guy you were getting ready to marry, then you should not have married him. Now, what? Money lost to pay the lawyers, slander, and a divorce. What would have happened to the kids if we had kids? I guess they get to suffer the most? What about the kids," replied Michael with a smile on his face!!! "Move away from the door Michael, Karina replied. "What did you say," said Michael? Then the door flew open and hit him in the face as Karina walked out of the bedroom with her bathing suit on and headed towards their Olympic sized swimming pool.

After Michael collected himself from the floor he followed her and asked, "No answer, what am I not good enough? I bring home the bacon. I do not cheat or make you work and suck off your money? Help you out do the dishes and treat you right. If you had a child you know I would stick around and take care of the baby, right," Michael asked? "Yes," Karina replied. Then what is your big problem with me? I did not try to set it up so Jolene and Jake would meet last night. I just thought that since you ladies were having a night out. I would take Jake and Brad out to a different spot then even you ladies would go to but I ended up picking the one spot you ladies decided to go to."

Karina was about to dive in the pool but before she did, she answered Michael. "If you really want to know why women ask for a divorce more than men do, well here it is. Yes, I guess most women are stupid because we did not think about how if they had kids with the guy, the children would end up growing up to become a stupid, immature, idiot from watching their father act like one!" Then Karina dived in the pool.

Michael instantly had a look of bewilderment on his face after being utterly blown away by Karina's statement. Then he replied, "Wow, speaking of immaturity. I did not disserve that immature comment," he said as Karina came up out of the water with no reply.

Silence fell between Karina and Michael until a cell phone ring came from inside the house. Michael ran inside to answer the phone. He picked up the phone to find Deseray on the other end. Then he walked the phone over to Karina, who had just got out of the pool, and was drying off. Karina asked, "Who is on the phone?" Michael answered, "It's the women that you convinced her to leave her nice guy boyfriend, who was good for her, for a one night stand, and a possible baby to raise by herself. Great advice Karina! I do not think a women who has just lost the love of her life to murder needs that headache," while handing her the phone.

Finally, Karina snapped and kicked Michael in the mid-section sending him crashing to the ground in pain letting the phone fall out of his hands. However, Karina caught the phone before it could hit the ground. Then she walked away laughing as she was greeting Deseray on the other end leaving Michael in pain on the ground saying to himself, "Well, I guess I deserved that."

CHAPTER 11

The Break

Early the morning after the murder Marc walked into the police station and down to the morgue to talk to the medical examiner about the body. The examiner told him the name of the victim was Don Mercer. She also told him that there was nothing special about this victim. His throat was just slit, nothing that she has never seen before. Marc replied, "Well all we need to do now is establish a motive and find the murder weapon." Then he walked upstairs to his office.

When he walked into his office he made a fresh cup of coffee and sat down at his desk to check the computer database for information on Don Mercer. The computer screen showed that he had been married to his wife of twelve years Monica and has two children one named Valerie who was four and another named Evan who was three. He had worked for city hall in the finance department twenty years. Then there was also an assault charge that was dropped seventeen years ago because it was settled out of court.

Marc suddenly looked up from the computer to find the coffee was done and poured himself a cup adding a teaspoon of sugar with some

Irish cream creamer. Then Officer Brennonhan walked into Marc's office. "How was the strip club? Being a young man there must have been fun. Get any free lap dances at the club?

"Ha, Ha, lame," Officer Brennonhan said with a pause afterwards. "Monica is here and so is Mrs. Shoeshiner, (otherwise known as Linda),"said Brennonhan. "Oh, trying to change the subject, huh. Do not want to answer or am I going to have to have to ask the strippers to answer that question myself? After a short pause Marc added, "Not answering, well then go question both women separately and then put them in the same room together as you ask some more questions. Do not tell either one that Linda was sleeping around with our unfaithful stiff. I want to be there to ask it when they are the same room together. It will make the day more interesting," Marc said. "We will also get to see whether or not they know each other or and if there is animosity between the two," replied Brennonhan.

5 MINUTES LATER

Marc walks out of his office to the observation room and begins to watch as Brennonhan brings Monica into the interrogation room. Monica sits down in the chair at the table as Officer Brennonhan leaves the room. Monica is a five foot eight inches. woman with a domino complexion wearing a pearl necklace and a black dress, weighing about one hundred twenty-five pounds. She also does not like to deal with peoples problems or give them any of hers as well.

While Marc enjoys his view of the woman through the glass between the viewing and interrogation rooms Officer Brennonhan opens the door to the viewing room and walks in. Standing behind Marc he asked, "Like the view?" Marc replies, "Not as good of a view as you just had. Better go get a better one." As Marc turned to exit the door and go to the interrogation room Brennonhan said, "Your right, the two women (having no idea who each one of them is) were sitting next to each other getting along just fine talking to one another in the waiting room." "Did Monica talk about her kids," asked Marc? "Yes, if there is a fight; my money is on the blond," replied Brennonhan. "Of course that is just like you to take the stripper; you're on," Marc said as he exited the room to start the interrogation.

"Good afternoon Mrs. Mercer. My name is Detective Skylark. I know you are going through a tough situation right now but I need you to try your best to tell me the story of what was going on the last couple of days before your husband's death," said Marc. "Where do I need to start," asked Monica Mercer? "Start with the last morning you spent with him and go back a week so you can end on a good note," answered Marc. "Ok, well here we go," Monica said in reply."

After a slight pause, Mrs. Mercer recalled the last day in this fashion. "I woke up as Don was getting ready for work for the city at the local government office. I asked him when he would be back and he said 5:30 PM. Then I got up and walked into the kitchen to make myself breakfast," she said.

Monica paused for a second to grab a drink of water Marc had poured for her. Then she continued saying, "Noticing the fact that there was very little milk in the fridge, I asked Don to grab some milk before he came home. He told me to give him some money since I make so much staying at home with the children. I threw some watermelon at him and told him to get out of the house and not to come back without the milk. Laughing, we kissed each other goodbye. Then he left for work and that was the last time that is saw him."

"Did you see activity that might have looked a little bit suspect to you or notice any activities that were different from any other day," Marc asked? "No, Don was the same he was always. Nothing new was going on," Monica replied. "Well, how was the rest of the week," asked Marc?

"Just like everyone else's week. Don went to work. I took the kids to school and picked them up. Cooking, cleaning, all that fun stuff that everyone hates doing but does it to survive unless you are a cook. Shopping in the middle of the week was the only way I could get some relief from the boredom of the daily routine before the children came home. The only setback I saw was in the middle of the week." "What was that," Marc replied? "Don came home from work and started complaining about how his boss was making him do something he did not want to do but I told him to stop complaining and that I did not want to hear it?"

With that said, Marc thought no there is no way that went over well as Monica continued her story. "Don's voice started to get louder and he said that he does not understand why every time that he has a problem that I do not want to hear about it. However, when you have a problem I have to listen to it and be you're emotional dump. That is all the respect I get while you get the whole day to yourself maybe doing two to three hours worth of cooking, cleaning, and picking up the kids at the school. Meanwhile, I work 10 or more hours a day six days a week and you can go out shopping and hanging with your unmarried friends that tell you all their nice stories about how their marriages and relationships suck. On top of that some of them are sleeping around with different men. Well maybe we should get a divorce since you think married life sucks so much and you can go sleeping around with different guys and live on welfare while working a job with two kids while I pay child support," said Mrs. Mercer.

"What happened after that explosion," Marc asked? "He left the room and went up to bed. I should have listened more to him and respected his feelings," she said as she started to cry. Then Marc leaned over hugging her telling her that everything will be alright and that his wife died so he knows where she is coming from.

After the interrogation Marc walked into the listening room as Monica left the police station. Officer Brennonhan inquired, "Are you going to tell her about the stripper?" "I do not know if that will be a good idea. Besides she thinks highly of him and that means her kids probably do too. The children do not need to know this neither does their mother. Even though he was not a saint I do not think the children need to know especially the son," replied Marc. "Why not isn't it best for them to know the truth about who their dad really was, a cheater, so they do not become like him, asked Brennonhan?" Then they both started to leave the listening room and walked into the hallways of the police station.

"Look I know what I said but in this case it is probably best we leave this subject alone. I was looking on the computer today at the Mercer file and the file said that his children were two and three years of age. If that is the case maybe they are still young enough to not understand what is going on. Also maybe if I have to end up telling Monica because of the case, (if we find the murderer) goes to trial, she will not tell the children because she does not want them to know about their father. Therefore, they will not think of why he did it and possible go on to commit the same offenses the father did. They may even get a new father who is actually a good role model for the children that will not have to compete with all the good and bad memories of their dad. On top of all of this, what man stepping into that situation would want to deal with the children not trusting him because their father cheated," said Marc?

"No wonder he cheated. If it were me I would not have cheated but I would have left her and told her good luck finding another man that would not treat her like she treated me. That definitely would have happened before we were married. What man would want to deal with a woman that dumps all her problems on him and does not care about his anyway," replied Officer Brennonhan? "Let's put it this way. It looks like she learned her lesson. Now she has to deal with the consequences. Maybe she will show some more love to the next guy instead of dumping on him and pushing him away. Then maybe he won't cheat. I am not saying what he did is right but if he was not getting the love and respect from his wife at home so he was probably going to end up cheating, separated, or getting a divorced anyway. That may be the only way for this man to get the love and respect he wants," was Mark's reply to that comment. "Looks like one of us has to go down to the city financial building and talk to Don's boss. Which one of us is it going to be," asked Brennonhan? "You get the stripper and I will head uptown. I am sick of interviewing people that cannot work a real nine to five. Besides, who has the background with the strippers? I sent you there last night do not tell me you did not take an opportunity to get a lap dance?" "You need to grow up," replied Officer Brennonhan. "You need to get a sense of humor Brennonhan," Marc said as he pointed his finger at Officer Brennonhan while leaving to go to city financial department with everyone laughing at Officer Brennonhan.

Meanwhile, at the harbor in New York an underwater welder was working when he found a knife lying on the rocks below him in the water. After he surfaced and he packed up to go home he cleaned off the knife and decided to keep it. Due to the fact that it was Friday night so he went home.

After he got home he ordered some Chinese takeout and a movie. Then he packed up for his fishing trip, sat down for a beer and Chinese food while he watched the movie. Then he went to sleep.

The next morning the welder drove to Pennsylvania to meet his friend to go fishing. When he got to the Susquehanna River he walked up to a yacht and Marc emerged from it with a smile on his face. "Hey how was the trip Keaton," asked Marc? "It was a good six hours," replied Keaton. "Well get you're fishing gear and let's go."

Two hours later, Keaton caught a rock fish. Then they started to cut open the fish with the knife that Keaton had found while welding. Marc noticed how the knife cut just like the one that slit Don's throat. Marc then asked, "Where did you find that at?" "I was welding at my job and found that underwater on a rock, said Keaton." "Can I take that to the police lab because it cuts the same way that a knife from one of our cases cuts. Do not worry I know you did not do it. The knife probably got dumped there by the killer or killers. I am just taking a hunch on this one," said Marc. "Ok, you can go ahead and take it but I bet you $100.00 it gets you nowhere in your case," said Keaton." "You're on," replied Mark! After the conversation ended Keaton handed Marc the knife then they went back to fishing.

CHAPTER 12

Dark, Wet, and Crazy Nights In Italy

A newly married Italian couple, roll off of each other after just having sex in their Venice motel room. The blond wife looks over at the clock to see it is five thirty in the afternoon. Then she turned over to her husband and said, "I am going to get ready and go to the masquerade ball. Then I will meet our friends from last night at the restaurant." "I will meet you there later," replied the husband. The wife went and took a shower. After she got out of the shower she put on a new dress. Then she grabbed her purse and quickly left the room.

Meanwhile, in another motel a couple blocks away another Italian man named Mr. Esposito was waiting for his wife to get dressed for the masquerade ball. The same masquerade ball as the newly married couple was going to. The wife asks, "Do you want to order in or out?" "How about I go walk around town for a while and find a place to eat? That will give you some time to get ready for the ball while I find a place to eat, replied the husband." "Ok, just give me a call in an hour with the name of the restaurant we will meet at," answered the wife. Then the husband left the motel and walked over to a motel a few blocks away."

When Mr. Esposito walked into the motel he went up the elevator to room 210. Then he knocked on the door. "Come in," a female voice said. He walked into a dark room turned the light on to see Mrs. Rossi (the newly married Italian wife that supposedly was going to meet her friends at a restaurant), naked on the bed. "Well hurry up and get undressed we do not have much time," Mrs. Rossi said. Then Mr. Esposito tore his clothes off and got in bed with her asking her what was a name of a good restaurant in the area.

Forty five minutes later Mr. Esposito called his wife and told her to meet him at the local wine cellar for dinner. Then he told Mrs. Rossi that he would see her tonight at the masquerade ball. Mrs. Rossi hung around the motel for a little while longer because she did not want to be anywhere near her husband. She did not love him but he loved her. She was in the relationship for the money. Plus, she did not like what he did for a living. Her husband was a so called banker but in reality he was also covering up for money laundering for the mafia.

However, what she really wanted to do was let him take her on extravagant vacation getaways and buy her expensive things. Then her next trick would be to get pregnant with his child and after the first Christmas with the child she would leave him. After that she would divorce him for irreconcilable differences. Keeping the child because she knows as long as she is a good mother she will be awarded the child by the courts. Therefore, she would be allowed to keep one of his cars, a decent amount of his money and get child support (or so she thinks). Until then she figures she will just screw around a little.

Arriving at the ball with her mask on, Mrs. Rossi starts looking for her friends the Espositos. While walking through the ballroom she grabs a glass of champagne off of a caterer's tray and heads toward the bar to order some tequila.

While waiting, she downed her glass of champagne. As soon as she received her shot of tequila she downed it and started walking over to some tables looking for the Espositos. At about the third table she walked to she saw the Espositos sitting with her husband Antonio Rossi. "Why you look like you're a little bit tipsy hun," said Mrs. Esposito. "Do not worry I am good to go. How about getting me another bottle of champagne Antonio," Mrs. Rossi replied while turning to her husband. "Like I said earlier my wife is always the life of the party," said Antonio as he was leaving to get some more champagne.

While Mr. Rossi was away the three friends talked about all the latest events that were happening throughout Europe and what the Rossi's had done on their honeymoon. The Espositos talked about the local soccer club game they had attended as well as skiing in the Dolomites. When they stopped talking about the game Mrs. Rossi started talking about the day her husband and her spent shopping for art. Then Mr. Rossi returned with the bottle of champagne she had asked for. "Thanks, let's go dancing," she replied.

Both couples made their way to the dance floor. After dancing a while they switched partners and continued to dance into the night. Around 10 o'clock Mrs. Rossi became tired and wanted to sit down to regain some strength.

After going back to the table Mr. and Mrs. Rossi started talking until she got bored with the conversation then suddenly she said, "Why don't you go enjoy dancing with your friends. I will catch up in a minute.

Mr. Rossi went back to the dance floor to join his friends. In the meantime a Mrs. Rossi had a couple drinks of champagne. Then she went to the bar to get another shot of some hard liquor. As she was waiting for her drink, a man in a devils mask with black hair stepped up and introduced himself to her asking her to dance. "Yes, but let me take another shot here first," she answered. "I will meet you on the dance floor in five minutes," he replied.

When Mrs. Rossi finished her shot she hurried to the dance floor finding the man in the devils mask with black hair. While they danced he whispered compliments and talked to her about the different sites he had seen and adventures he had embarked upon in his lifetime. Then she took him to meet her friends and her husband at the table they were sitting at.

Another hour of talking and dancing had gone by and the man in the devils mask excused himself from the group and left. Upon the man leaving the Rossi's and the Espositos took to the dance floor again.

Twenty minutes went by and Mrs. Rossi told her husband she was sick and decided to go back to the hotel. Her husband who was having such a good time at the masquerade ball did not follow.

During her walk down the streets of Venice Mrs. Rossi could hear her footsteps echoing off the houses and the canal ways. At first she heard only her footsteps. Then she heard a second pair of footsteps walking through the dark alleyways. Mrs. Rossi started to follow them. Looking down each alleyway till she could no longer hear them. She started to smile thinking, "He has to be close."

Finally, as Mrs. Rossi passed by yet another alleyway someone grabbed her and pulled her into the dark alleyway. Seeing the man in the devils mask with black hair she smiled pulled up his mask to see his face (that was covered by the darkness of the alleyway so that no one other than her could see his face) and kissed him. Then he swung her around lifted up her skirt as he leaned her up against the wall in the alley and started to have sex with her. After a while Mrs. Rossi leaned back against him kissing him until they both came to an orgasm. Then they got dressed and walked to his hotel room. Where upon opening the door for her, he knocked her out with chloroform.

When Mrs. Rossi woke up and the effects of the chloroform gave away she realized she was sitting down in another dark alleyway. The alley led to the street and at the end of the street was a canal. Then as her mind started to clear more she realized her mouth was taped, while she wore a fur coat on her.

Trying to stand up on two feet the man with the devil's mask with black hair grabbed her and put a gun in her back saying, "Run up and down the alley till I say to stop. Do not pull off the tape from your mouth." Mrs. Rossi ran up and down the alleyway till her skin started to burn. Then she jumped in the water to try and stop the burning. The man in the mask was smiling as he walked up to her. Seeing the pain she was in he said to her, "By the way if you have not figured out by now there is a chemical that reacts with your body heat in the fur coat but I will put you out of your misery now. Then he pushed her head into the water till she drowned.

About lunchtime the next day, the detective working the Mrs.

Rossi case led Mr. Rossi into the morgue to identify his wife Teresa Rossi's body. When he saw the body he said, "Yes, that is her." Then the mortician and the detective left Mr. Rossi and his wife alone.

Two days later the autopsy was done and the detective called Mr. Rossi into the police station. Once Mr. Rossi entered the detective's office the detective said, "You're not going to like what I have to tell you but we think your wife was sleeping around on you." "Well that is not totally surprising the way people are now and days. Why, do you think that", asked Mr. Rossi? "Well, we found a cocktail of sperm from different people your wife slept with. Could you tell me the events of your honeymoon," asked the detective?

After Mr. Rossi and the detective were finished talking Mr. Rossi left. The detective pulled out his cell phone and dialed up one of the officers working the case telling him to bring Mr. and Mrs. Esposito in for questioning as well as the man in the devils mask with the black hair. When the Espositos walked in he questioned both of them in separate rooms then together. Finally, after two hours of questioning them he let them leave.

Then the detective turned to one of his officers and said, "I told the wife I cannot prove it but I think her husband was sleeping with Mrs. Rossi. She did not flip out or anything but cried and said that she had no idea other than the fact that the times she said she was alone matched up with when Mr. Rossi said he was alone. "Did you find the man in the devils mask with black hair," the officer asked? "No, we are checking hotels in the area to see if anyone checked out abruptly though," replied the detective.

After that Marc turned his attention to crime scene. "Did you find any evidence from the crime scene," asked the detective. "Well the burns on Teresa Rossi's body were defiantly from chemicals that are sold around here but they were mixed in a cocktail just like the sperm was to," said the officer. "See if there is any video equipment or bugs in the Esposito's or in the Rossi's motel rooms. Have you figured out anything about the word whore that was written on the alley wall, at Mrs. Rossi's murder scene asked the detective," "No," replied the officer.

Meanwhile, up in the Dolomites of Italy a young couple was

checking into a ski resort. Upon receiving their key they were shown to their room and they entered into their quarters giving the bag boy a tip as he left. Then the woman exhausted from a night out in Venice at an art show, walked into the bedroom to catch some sleep. "Man I am exhausted. How about you come take a little nap with me," she said to her lover while motioning him to the bed with her finger and a seductive look? Exhausted himself he pulled off his shirt (to reveal his well sculpted shoulder and abs) walked into the bedroom (with a smile) shutting the doors behind him.

At about 3:00 PM they both went to get massages and then they went to do a workout. First, they ran three miles around the indoor track. Then they hit the weight room listening to a mix of metal, club, dance, and hip hop music. When they were finished they hit the showers and went swimming for a while. Finally, they ordered dinner for two in their room where they had veal parmesan, lasagna, wine, and the desert being sex in the hot tub out on the balcony as the sun went down with a view of the mountains in the background.

Early in the afternoon the next day the couple, Christian and Maria began cross country skiing to see some of the wildlife. About an hour later they ran into an injured skier. While, calling emergency services they waited with the blonde hair women from America. "What are you doing out here alone, said Maria?" "I wanted to go to Europe for my birthday but my husband did not so he paid for me to go by myself. Could you guys call my husband for me and tell him what happened and that I may be here longer," replied the women?" "Yes," answered Maria. Then the rescue crews appeared in a helicopter taking the women away.

After that the couple skied back to the resort. At the resort they took a shower and went to lunch at the restaurant there. While they were at the restaurant they ordered Stromboli and talked about the injured women, as well as the art they had seen in Venice two days ago.

"Did you see the gash on that women's leg," said Maria. "Yes, I wonder how she is doing," replied Christian? "Probably not to well considering she hit a tree," answered Maria. "Why does it always have to be a tree," asked Christian? "Yeah, you always hear of skiers hitting a tree on the news," replied Maria. "Must be a slow news day, why can they not talk about something good for once," asked Christian? "Ratings equals money, that's seems to be all the news stations care about these days. The only way a person can get on the news any more is by saving a life, sport achievements, something illegal, hurting someone, or if that person is doing something that the people doing the news like," replied Maria. "I agree sounds pretty selfish to me," replied Christian. Maria replied by nodding her head yes and changed the subject of the conversation to the art they had seen in the show the other day till lunch ended.

Upon ending dinner the couple left to go take a nap in their room. After about two hours of sleeping our couple woke up to knocking on the door of their room. Christian opened the door and standing outside the door was the woman that was injured while skiing. She was on crutches. Then she invited them to dinner saying that she would like to repay them for their good deed and they turned her down. However, the woman was persistent so they reconsidered.

Later, that night at dinner Maria talked with the injured women. "We never got your name. What is it," Maria asked? "Janet Lieberum," she answered. "What did the doctors say about your leg Janet," asked Maria. "Believe it or not, all I need is some stitches. I did not break, dislocate, or pull anything. What did my husband say," replied Janet? "He asked if you wanted him to come here and if you needed anything," Christian said. "Well after dinner I will have to call him," said Janet. The conversation changed to another subject then continued till dinner was over.

The next morning was uneventful but the afternoon was not. Maria went to a local town shopping while Christian worked out. When she was done shopping for some snacks and drinks she passed a clothing store and bought some lingerie. In the meantime Christian had meet a tall five foot ten inch blonde haired women while working out and took her back to the Jacuzzi at Maria and Christian's balcony outside their room.

When Maria got back she opened the door to her room and sat the food and lingerie on the bed. She then looked up to see the blonde and Christian kissing in the Jacuzzi. Then she walked outside shutting the door behind her slowly so that they would not notice her. As she shut the door Maria started to cry and left the resort to check into another one.

Walking out of the resort she went to a motorcycle rental store and as she walked in she started to smile thinking, At least I have his credit card. Then she walked in looked up and saw a black leather motorcycle jacket and pants. Taking them off the rack she walked into the dressing room and tried them on.

Minutes later Maria walked out of the dressing room bought the black leather motorcycle, jacket, pants, and a matching helmet. Then she rented a red and black motorcycle for three days, which was all on Christian's credit card of course. Finally, after spending over 700 Euro's she left.

Arriving at the other resort Maria checked into her room. Then she walked down to the bar in the resort. "This round is on me," said Maria to everyone at the bar and handing her now ex's credit card to the bartender. Not long after she sat down a man with black hair and blue eyes walked in the bar and sat down next to her asking if this seat was taken. She answered, "No," and continued drinking. "What's wrong a man," he said? "Oh yeah how could you tell, the frown on my face," Maria replied? "Been there," he replied. "Oh, you mean with a guy," she said. "Hell no," he replied. "So then you must go both ways," she said with a laugh. Then he started to laugh.

After a momentary pause Maria asked, "Ok then, cut the crap. What is it you want the money, the girl, or both?" "I do not need either, I already have money and I can get just about any woman I want. You looked sad, so I just wanted to cheer you up. You know give you someone to talk to, but maybe I should just take my drink and go somewhere else. If this is all I get for being a nice guy," the man with the black hair and blue eyes replied?

However, after he started to walk away Maria felt sorry (not to mention she was attracted to him as well) and said, "I am sorry. If that is all, excuse my rudeness and sit back down, please." The man said nothing, walked over and sat down at a table in the back of the room, near the stage. Maria left the bar and followed him over to where he was sitting to sit next to him.

"What do you do for a living," Maria asked. "I own stocks in several companies," answered the blue eyed man. "What type of companies," Maria asked. "Solar power, shale fracking, coffee, tent manufacturing, and Japanese cars," the man replied. "That's pretty smart betting on both sides of the political spectrum but why tents may I ask," replied Maria? "Simple more homeless people living on the streets. If economy starts to get better I will sell the stock," he replied.

Conversations between the two went throughout the night and continued as the dark hair blue eyed man walked her to her room. When they got to her room she asked him to come in for a little nightcap but he declined. Before he walked away she asked, "What is your name?" "Thomas Swanky," he replied. She giggled and said, "Have a nice night see you at breakfast tomorrow."

Early next morning Maria met Thomas for breakfast then they went cross country skiing. Finally, they went back and spent some time in the hot tube in her room before lunch. Maria asked him if he wanted to have lunch in her room and he said, "Of course." "I am going to take a shower first. You order lunch. When I get out you can shower while I wait for the food," said Maria.

After Thomas got out of the shower he could hear a noise coming from the bedroom. As he walked into the room he saw Maria shredding a credit card. "Your old boyfriend's," he asked? "That and over 800 Euro's on his card is what he gets for cheating on me," she said as the room service knocked on the door.

Upon entering the room with the service cart Thomas and Maria checked out the food, tipped the room service, and started to eat. Thomas ate some veal parmesan and she had some prime rib with apples and mushrooms. Then they watched some TV for a while and took a nap until later that afternoon when they woke up. Then they woke up and went to the weight room to work out. After that they jumped into the pool. Finally, they ended their day in the shower together.

After that the new couple headed to dinner in the resort. They went out to town to ice skating as well. Then they had some coffee and desert, followed by some conversation. Fascinated with Thomas; Maria started talking about her family at home.

Maria told Thomas about her job working for a cigarette company and had stock in the company as well as American Oil Company in Russia. She also told him how she had a sister at home that was a model that was also an artist back in the city of Millan. "Looks like you will have to introduce me to her someday," replied Thomas with a smile. Maria in turn punched him in the shoulder and told him to shut up. Thomas replied by bursting out in laughter at her.

Then Maria started talking about her parents and how they owned a flower shop in Millan. "They have been married for twenty-five years," she said as she started to cry. "What's wrong," Thomas asked? "Mom wanted to meet Christian (the reason being was, he had money because he was a pediatrician) and I was looking forward to introducing them to each other for the first time. I also thought that maybe he would propose to me here but I was wrong. How could I be so stupid to think my dream man that was so hansom and kind hearted would want anything with me other than use me for sex or is it something I did to chase him away? Why am I always screwing things up? What is wrong with me," Maria said as she continued to cry?

"There is nothing wrong with you hon. Christian just does not understanding what a sweet, fun loving, and beautiful woman he had. He is the one with the problem not you," replied Thomas.

After a slight pause Thomas went on to say, "Look in my travels I have meet many nice people beautiful women and handsome men that are not like Christian. They are one out of every five but there are billions of people in this world. You are bound to find someone if you do not give up. Maybe we will work out."

Pausing again Maria asked, "Would you like to come over to my room for some coffee and cake?" "Yes, what type of cake are we having," he said as they got up to leave? "German chocolate cake sound good," she asked. "Sure," he answered as they walked down the hallway to her room.

When the couple entered the room Maria called in an order for German Chocolate cake as Thomas made some Brazilian bold coffee. As soon as Maria was finished she walked over putting her arms around Thomas, kissed him, then said, "What you want to go all night long or something?" "Something, look I am not trying to take advantage of you and have sex with you so quickly after you just broke it off with your man. I am not like that, understood," Thomas replied? "Yes, that does not mean you cannot spend the night here with me. Fair enough," she answered?" "Fair," he replied.

After they had some cake and coffee they laid next to each other on the bed watching movies and talking most the night. Finally, Maria nodded off; causing Thomas to kiss her on the forehead, turn off the TV, and fall asleep.

The next morning Thomas woke up and looked over to see Maria was not there. He got up looked around the room to see no one was there. Upon seeing her absence he got dressed and walked to the resorts dining facilities and ordered breakfast. While eating breakfast he thought maybe she wanted some alone time or she went back to her old boyfriend.

Thomas was right Maria did go back to see her ex but only to tell him off. When she was finished (after thirty minutes of arguing) she said, "Well Christian I have found someone better and I never want to see you again." Then she zipped up her leather suit, put on her black helmet, got on her motorcycle, and took off down the mountain roads to her resort.

Christian having thought about how he still loved her he chased after her on his motorcycle. However, she got too far out ahead of him and he lost sight of her around a corner. Undeterred however he kept chasing and started to catch her. Unfortunately, he ran into a tripwire throwing him from his bike and his head hit a rock knocking him unconscious.

Christian woke up inside a dark room tied to a chair. Then the light came on and a dark figured with a voice that sounded like it was being altered through a machine appeared holding a container of green liquid. "Looks like you screwed with the wrong girl this time. Trash like you does not deserve to live. Too bad your sight is to blurred by the chemicals I have running through the air to see me. You would be so surprised to see who it is," the figure said. Then the dark figure stepped up to him in a gas mask and poured acid down his throat. After listening to the screams stop the figure poured acid all over Christian's body and took whatever was left and threw it into an incinerator. Following this up the killer gave the floor a good cleaning.

Hours later Maria woke up lying on a graded metal floor in a warehouse that was not lit well. Feeling something crawl across her leg, Maria flicked it off of her not knowing what it was and got up. She started to walk over into the light to try to orient herself and figure out where she was. As she walked into the light she felt something crawl on her again she flicked it off of her. Then looked down and saw inside the metal grading spider webs with hundreds of spiders crawling across them and up her legs. Then she started to scream and knock the spiders off of her until the spider venom from the bites overtook her.

One day later, Thomas walked into a police station looking at his watch to make sure Maria was gone forty-eight hours to file the missing persons report. An hour later he was done and he said that if they needed to talk to him in person that he would be in the country six more days then he would head back to the states. Afterwards he left his United States phone number he left the resort.

CHAPTER 13

The Weekend and Holiday Is Over

With the holiday weekend begin over. A manager of major trucking company stands outside the business yawning and stretching his arms up in the air at the same time, holding the key to the business in his hand. He opens the door and turns the light switch on. After the light turns on he looks up towards the trucks and the belt that is used to help load the trucks, where there is a spider so far off in the distance he cannot see it. Not seeing the spider (that starts to run underneath one of the trucks) he shuts the door and takes his normal walk to the office half way a crossed the building. He puts the identification code into the door to the office. Then he opens the door and turns the light on. Finally, starts to walk to his desk. As the door shuts behind him a spider starts crawling up the wall behind him.

Making an attempt to sit down at his desks the manager hears a scream of a woman come from the belt. Running out the door of the office and to the belt the manager starts to hear screams for his name. When he gets up the stairs to the start of the belt he sees his secretary covering her mouth crying as she points down at the dead body on the graded walk way. The body was Maria's covered with spider webs and spiders crawling all over her body.

Once again the same detective that is working on the Rossi murder walked onto the crime scene to see another dead body. Looking at the body of Maria he thinks to himself, "Two grotesque murders in a row. Hope this is just a coincident and not a serial killer?" Then he turned to his assistant and said sarcastically, "Wonderful, these spiders did not just randomly appear here out of nowhere. Especially after that last murder in Venice, when they hear about the fact there is possible a serial killer on the loose throughout Northern Italy people are going to freak out.

Back in the United States Marc did not waste any time going down to the lab to find out the results of the tests done on the knife Keaton found. When he got down to the lab he got the answer he wanted which was the knife cuts the same as the knife that killed Don Mercer. "Then lab technician said, "However, there were no finger prints on the knife so we cannot find the murderer off of that alone. From the way the knife cuts the knife could very well be the murder weapon so you know what to do next." "Well, then thank you for your time," replied Marc.

Five minutes later, Marc makes a phone call. "Keaton how are you!" said Marc. Boy you sound excited Marc. Let me guess, you found something on the knife. "Yes the knife is the same type of knife that killed Mr. Mercer but it is not enough for a conviction because there are no figure prints on it, said Marc. "Well that sucks Marc but something came of it so now I owe you. When and where do I pay up," said Keaton? Then Marc replied, "I will meet you at the restaurant but first tell me exactly where the place was you found the knife again?"

Meanwhile, Michael walked into the living room where Karina and Deseray were sitting. He had an important announcement to make. However, upon seeing Jolene Michael said, "What are you doing here," said Michael? Then after a pause he said, "You just show up out of nowhere all the time causing trouble!" Then Jolene jumped up out of her seat pulled a handgun out of her purse and ran a crossed the room putting the gun right under Michael's chin and angling it up towards his brain saying, "All right I am sick of you. You want to test?" Michael to a look at her in fear and said, "Yes, I am sick of your crap." Then she pulled the trigger Michael fell to the ground as the sound of the gun rang through the air.

Karina ran over to him screaming, "Michael," as she got over to him she noticed the smile on his face. At the same time she realized a sound kept coming from outside the house. Then everybody started laughing as Michael started to get up laughing himself. Karina slapped him upside the face called him a jerk (causing more laughter) and walked outside to see Brad with firecrackers all over the ground going off.

"I cannot believe you," Karina said to Brad. Then she said to Michael, "What is this about?" "I thought it would be funny to get you back for kicking me in the mid-section and I got tickets to India for our reunion this year."

Hours went by as the Michael and Karina's reunion party went deep into the night. After a couple of bottles of hard liquor were disposed of; a few games of cards, as well as a game of mafia were done. Jolene sat drinking some wine with Karina talking about Jake. "So how is that poor sap Jake doing," said Jolene? I do not know I have not seen him in a while. Talk to Michael," answered Karina.

Michael, (who was sitting across from them) looked up and said, "Oh it's the same crap every day, up to his same old womanizing ways. Other than that he is a nice guy." To which Deseray replied, "You mean same serial killer ways?" Then she went to the bathroom.

Karina then gave Michael an evil stare and said, "Wait ago Michael," and went to the bathroom to talk to Deseray. "Hey Michael wait ago Mike," Jolene said to him sarcastically and started laughing. Michael did not reply he just shook his head at her. Then Jolene finished off her glass of wine and reached for the bottle to find out there was no more. Then she looked at her watch "Oh no, looks like it is too late to get the hard stuff looks like I will have to get the cheap junk at the gas station," said Jolene. "I will drive, your too the gas station," said Michael. "Might as well. You already killed the mood, you worthless fool. Since you cannot do anything else right, you might as well make yourself useful by driving me to get some more beer." she replied. Then they got up and started to walk towards the door. "Michael, Jolene said. "Yes," Michael replied with a sigh! "Don't screw this up," Jolene said and started to laugh as they exited the house.

When they got to the store Jolene walked in and went to the refrigerators with the beer in them. She opened the door to the fridge grabbed a twenty-four pack and shut the door only to turn to find Jake standing right there staring at her. "Kate what is wrong with you," he said to her? "She looked at him with a weird look and said, "Who the hell are you?" Jake replied, "Don't give me that crap Kate!" "Look obviously whoever this Kate is she really pissed you off because you have a really stern voice right now but if you do not leave me alone I will call the cops sir and if that does not work." Then she flashed the gun in her purse. Jake stood there for a second as Jolene turned around and started to walk away. However, when Jolene reached the counter Jake said, "Ok then what is your name?" Jolene looked up with a stern look on her face and said, "Gina, now do not test me or else."

After seeing this episode erupt in front of him, the store clerk said, "Sir, if you do not leave the poor women alone I am going to have to ask you to leave." Do not worry sir you have nothing to worry about from me," replied Jake.

When the transaction was approved by clerk Jolene, looked at Jake and said, "Do not try to follow me or you're going to get shot." Then she walked out the door with the twenty-four pack in her hand. Once she got into the car she said, "Jake is in there. Let's go!" Michael put the car in in reverse pulled out their parking spot and left.

Later, that night around 4:00 AM Marc and Officer Brennonhan were sitting in a pickup truck by the docks in the New York Harbor at the same place Keanon had found the knife. When suddenly, a man in a trench coat came up to the docks and lit a cigarette. Marc said, "Finally, something is going on, looks like we will have to wait a little longer." After about fifteen minutes of watching from a distance another man walks up to the man in the trench coat and a drug deal ensues. "Good now we have leverage," said Brennonhan. "Just make sure he makes the exchange first," replied Marc.

Two minutes went by and the two criminals finally made the trade.

Before they walked away Marc and Officer Brennonhan stepped out the truck and said you're both under arrest. The man with the bag of roofies started to run while the dealer just stood there. Officer Brennohan yelled at the man running, "Do not make me pull my gun. I will shoot you in the back." Hearing these words the man stopped, turned around, walked back, and got read his Miranda rights to him by Marc, while the dealer was put in cuffs and read his rights by Officer Brennonhan.

CHAPTER 14

Weeks' Worth Of Surprises

"Well I got you for buying roofies. You also got a nice little past behind you to. Caught stealing cars, raping an eighteen year old girl, and the funniest one of all, soliciting an undercover cop for sex," Marc said while laughing. "You are pretty dumb man so let's see how dumb you are. I have decided to offer you a deal and with a little bit of information as well as some cooperation I could have you back on the streets in no time charges dropped. However, I want you to stay away from the little girls or next time I see you I could make you wish I killed you instead of thrown you in jail and I know the courts will be on my side. No one likes a piece of crap like you. Maybe I will just castrate you or something. I do not know yet. The jury will imagine their daughters (if they have any) being touched by someone as sick as you and if they could they would suggest the most horrendous death possible," said Marc now yelling at the criminal named Clay.

"You know what the murders in jails to do to little rapists like you?" said Marc. "No sir," said the convicted rapist. "First they will probably rape you then eventually after they have had enough fun with you they gut you! You sick peace of crap," said Marc. Then after a couple of moments Marc finished by yelling, "Well you haven't made your mind up yet! Ok, I will give you some time to make your mind up sitting next to a guy over night that is surely going to get convicted of murder for killing a punk like you who messed with his daughter." Ok, I will take the deal," the rapist said in a hurry! This gave Marc a smile. Then Marc replied laughing, "Man you really are stupid. I would have chosen to cooperate in a hurry. That's the difference between the two of us."

"Well then here is the deal I got for you last weekend a man's throat was slit and a wife became a widow. The funny part was there was no knife, until of course; it was found right off the same pier you were getting your roofies at. Yeah, I know it sucks don't it one man or men screw up and I ruin your sick twisted head's good night cap plan so here is what you are going to do. First, you are going tell me if you have seen anyone suspect and then you are going to be my eyes and ears. On top of this you are going to help me arrest some of these criminals. You understand," asked Marc?

"I have been there to buy a couple of times but have seen no knife being thrown in the water. There are a lot of people that hang out by the docks down there," replied the Clay. "Good then, I am going to go get some pen and paper so you can write them down. You want coffee," asked Marc? "So now that I am cooperating with you you're going to give me stuff," said the criminal? The smile on Marc's face instantly straightened. Then he said, "Now do you want this or the jail cell with the guy who murdered a man for touching his little girl?" "One teaspoon of sugar cane and some milk," replied the criminal. "You're getting sugar. Criminals do not get the good stuff especially ones that mess with eighteen year old girls," Marc said while walking out of and slamming the door to the interrogation room.

While Marc walked down the hallway to get some coffee, paper and a pen; Officer Brennonhan walked up to ask what had happened. "Sounds like you had a lot of fun in there Detective Skylark," Brennonhan said. "Yes, I did. I did the world a favor and castrated him. Just imagine a person like that can still have kids, if he has not already had one. I will make sure his coffee is extra hot for when I pour it on his lap." "Just calm down," replied Officer Brennonhan. "I am still trying to find my daughter's dead boyfriend's killer and I have to deal with this crap. Just stop talking while you are ahead, so how did your interrogation go," said Marc. "The dealer is not talking without a lawyer," said the officer. "Figures," replied Marc as he grabbed for the coffee pot.

Later on that evening, the bank teller Maria went out to eat with Martin Benin. Then after dinner he took her in his limo to see a symphony orchestra in concert. When the concert was over he bought her some roses and took her on a Clydesdale ride. Then took her home to her place walked her to the door kissed her good night and left.

Meanwhile, in the evidence room under the cover of darkness a man walks in and grabs the knife used in the murder of Mr. Mercer out of the evidence locker then walks out of the building. The next day the lab technician walks into the room to do some more tests on the alleged murder weapon only to see the weapon is not there. Then she ran to tell Detective Skylark.

Two nights later sitting in a car at the same spot as the drug deal went down Marc talks to Officer Brennanhan and Clay (the criminal they caught in the drug deal). "So who are these people hanging around the docks right now," says Marc. "Mostly poor people and drug addicts," Clay replied. "Anyone important Marc," Marc asked? "No," replied Clay. "Well maybe Jolene is having better luck, right Jolene," said Marc into the head phone he had on? Jolene (who was now at a local night club around the docks there in New York) said all wired up, "Yes, Marc there are plenty of young druggies and dealers here. There is also plenty of young women hanging around with old men at this club here trying to get free drugs, alcohol, and money. Your single Marc maybe you should be here instead of me. Maybe you'll get some." "No I got plenty when I was married probably more than you will ever get with your one night stands. That sounds more your speed especially after you messing around with a guy that screws anything that has a pulse, "Jake." You get yourself checked hon after screwing with him you might as well just mess with anyone in that club." Brennonhan and Clay heard this and started laughing. "Alright old man, you know you would get with me if I gave you the chance," she replied. "Oh, come on a little girl like you who messes with little boys like Jake. Why would I stoop so low? It is below my standards. Remember your talking to a guy that stayed with his wife for sixteen years till her death. I bet most your relationships do not even last sixteen days so ask yourself, "Do you know what love is?" At this point everyone in the car was silent and everyone was listening to the conversation. After a moment of silence Jolene answers, "After this case is over you are going to pay old man."

Cracking a smile Marc replies, "Somehow I do not think so young lady." Then everyone in the car starts laughing. "Now let's get back to the topic at hand. Anything special going on there that can help us out with this case." "No, but it is open mic night and I have a pretty good voice, so I will grab some attention soon," answered Jolene.

While Jolene is singing her song Clay notices some people at the dock he has seen before at the club Jolene is currently at. "That is Lawrence and Alex who are bodyguards at the club. They are bodyguards for the club owner," he said. "What is his name," Marc asked? "Mr. Indescribable," Clay replied. Then Marc talked to Jolene after her song was over and said, "Did you hear what Clay said?" "Yes, I will work on that she replied, "Time to turn this recording device off and get rid of all this gear so I can try to gain some trust around here. See you Detective Skylark." Then there was silence.

Marc walks into the police station the next morning puts on a cup of coffee. Then he waits for Jolene to call in to tell him what happened last night. Marc picks up the morning paper sitting on his desk and starts to read the latest report on the murder. After a couple of minutes Marc gets up goes to get his cup of coffee, when his phone rings. He picks up the phone to hear Jolene on the other end. "Good morning Detective Skylark. How are you," she said? "Tired but not as tired as you sound," he answered. "Well let's get to too it. Last night I spent most of it club hoping with one of Mr. Indescribable's body guards. The champ was all up in my face most the night and I cannot believe how much he smokes. If he breathed on me one more time I think I would have to smack him around a little bit. However, he passed out after mixing a couple of shots with a line of cocaine. Then I searched his place and found nothing of any significance except for a receipt to a collectables store," Jolene said. "Well you check up on the store and see if there have been any sales of exotic knives as of lately and I think we have some growth here," replied Marc. "Well what do you mean," asked Jolene. "I am surprised you did not take advantage of the situation and get some," he answered. "Ok, you're just digging your grave ten times deeper. You remember what I did to Jake I can do ten times worse to you," she replied in anger! In reply, Marc just laughed at her words.

Walking into the collectable shop Jolene took a look around and waited till the store was empty of customers. Then she walked up to the register showed her badge and said that she needed to talk to the owner during lunch time when the shop closes for an hour. The cashier went and told the owner, after taking one look at her the owner agreed.

Three hours later at 1:00 PM the owner locked the door and turned around to see Jolene standing there staring at him, with a stern look on her face. Then the owner asked, "What do you want Miss?"

After pulling out a photo of the knife from the police lab the owner knowing exactly what she wanted, went over to his computer, and pulled up a picture with a description of the knife on it. "There were only about one hundred of these knives made in the world before making them was outlawed," he said. Then he pulled out a knife and brought out a manikin. "First, you stab the manikin, "as you see here." "First, you hit the button which is disguised as the emblem on the knife. After that the blade splits off into three blades inside the body curling out like fish hooks, having razor sharp blades attached above the hooks, so just imagine the damage that can be done to the body after that," the store owner asked? Jolene shook her head and asked, "You ever sold one of these?" "Yes one," he replied and he pointed to the computer screen. Jolene walked up to the screen wrote down the name and started to walk out the door. Then the owner said, "But wait there is more." He hit the emblem three times and hit the button again and the blades started to spine fast like a saw as if it was an assassin's weapon. After that he demonstrated that he could cut a manikin in half.

Two weeks later, the police role up into Mr. Indescribables club and arrested Kenny Dotson (also known as dice) and Jason Vetor (also known as Ace). "This is now a crime scene. You are all staying for questioning. Do not try to run all the doors are blocked. Especially you," Marc says pointing into a crowd of people. Two girls and a guy point at themselves. "No the dude with the traces of cocaine on his sleeve," Marc says. Then the man tried to run.

Officer Brennonhan, (who just happens to be standing by close to the man) pulls out his club, and throws it at the man's legs tripping him up causing him to fall strait to the floor. Officer Brennonhan then runs up and puts the man in the cuffs as he reads him his Miranda rights. The man fights back so Brennonhan beats him with the club a couple times till he stays down. Officer Brennonhan now starts to pick up the addict as another man starts to open his mouth to say, "That's police brutality!" To which Marc replies, "Sir, keep going and I will have you arrested for interfering with my police investigation and if you decide you want to get physical by hitting one of us. We can have you play a role in act two of the play that just ended on the floor!"

Just then the man that Officer Brennonhan had hand cuffed head bunted him and started running for the back door but before he could stop to grab the door to open it, the door swung open knocking him backward sending him crashing to the floor, smacking his head on the floor, effectively knocking him out as another police officer walked in the building.

As Officer Brennonhan went to revive the man so he could send him to the hospital to get checked out and on to jail." Marc made a statement to the crowd, "You see what happens when you run from us. Now, cooperate and do not make it hard on yourselves." Silence ensued as Officer Brennohan escorted the now conscious criminal outside to meet the ambulance.

Later on that night, after the police had left Mr. Indescribable's place they had a meeting in his back office. One of his employees asked, "So what are we going to do now?" "We are going to pay for the bail. Then take care of the problem the way we always do," Mr. Indescribable replied.

Two nights later Marc was driving home when he noticed the same car following him for fifteen minutes strait. Marc turned into a local rest stop on Route 30. He pulled his gun from underneath his seat and put it in his trench coat and hurried for the door of the rest stop. Once he was inside he ran directly into the women's restroom before the two people following him could see where he was going. After that he drew his gun and peaked out of the restroom to see where the two men were going. As he saw them enter the men's restroom drawing their guns. Then he ran out the front door of the rest stop and strait to his car to leave in a hurry. Pulling out onto the road he called Officer Brennonhan and Jolene telling them to meet him at his home.

When he pulled into the house he saw no cars there and the place was dark. He decides to enter around back. Where as soon as he opened the door a woman pulls him into house and throws him onto the floor. Marc looks up to see Deseray pointing a gun at his head. "Dad, why did you come in the back," she said. "I am being followed by men with guns. Probably the Mr. Indescribable's goons," he replied. Then Jolene and Officer Brennohan stepped out of the shadows with assault rifles. "Marc stands up and says to Jolene and Brennonhan, "In the basement I have some riot gear including stun grenades and tear gas. Go get some gas masks and stay in here. Deseray and I will go put some scopes on our hunting rifles. Then we will hide in the woods. Deseray and I will aim for whoever is going in the back door, while I will take care of whoever comes in the front. When they knock on the door, Jolene will scream that they have got guns so they will kick down the front door thinking they have surprised us. Then Officer Brennonhan and Jolene should have their masks on and throw some tear gas at them while we hit them. Then take care of it."

Ten minutes later two cars with tinted windows showed up. One parked out front the other parked out back. Five people jumped out of both cars. Two of them had sniper rifles. One ran to the woods out back. The other went to the woods in the front to post up to try to shoot anyone who may run out either door that was not one of them. All the others headed for the front door with automatic assault weapons and shoot guns.

Before Jolene could say anything the criminals blew off the door knob on both the front and the back door to begin the siege. However,

Deseray and Marc took two of them out before they got in the door. Marc and Deseray then went after the two men with sniper rifles.

Back inside the house after seeing the doors blasted and kicked open Jolene blew a big hole in the first guy's head that entered the door. Then she yelled gas while throwing the tear gas and put her mask on. Brennonhan threw his mask on then he shoot one of the criminals in the chest making a gaping wound. After that two of the goons dived outside the house trying to get away from the shoot gun blasts and started to crawl away from the house. Meanwhile, the other two ran and hide inside the house.

Back in the woods, Deseray and her dad hunted down the snipers. One of the snipers climbed up in a tree to get the drop on whomever he thought was hunting him down. The other went after Deseray.

Back inside the house the house Brennonhan and Jolene knew there was not much time before the tear gas would start to dissipate so they started hunting the two criminals that were still inside the house. First, they checked all the closets by blowing holes in each of the doors before they kicked them in. The result was Brennonhan kicked open one of the doors and it contained one of the goons lying dead with blood all over the clothes in the closet. The other one snuck up on Officer Brennonhan but Jolene knocked him out with the butt of her gun before he could shoot him. After that Jolene kicked the gun out of his hand and hewoke up and ran into another room. Then one of the criminals from outside reentered the house and shot her in the arm making her drop her weapon and dived to the floor to avoid another bullet. After that she rolled into the other room as the goon kept firing at her. Before the goon could make it into the room to shoot her she pulled a small pistol out her boot. Then he swung around the corner to shot her only to get a bullet right in the gut.

Meanwhile, Deseray hearing the guy chasing her from the distance while firing at her ran towards a nearby creek diving in. After swimming a while she got far enough away she hide standing in the water covered up by a bush that leaned over her down into the water causing the man to pass by not noticing her.

Later, the man in the tree decided to make a run for the car since from his view point he saw the gun fight was not going his way. The man made it to the car, sat down in the driver's seat and looked to see no keys in the ignition. Then Marc came running out of the woods and threw a stun grenade at him. The man eventually rolled out the door trying to drawl his gun. However, Marc had already pulled out a hand gun and had it pointed to his head. When the criminal would not stop drawing his gun Marc pulled the trigger.

When Marc finally made it back to the house the place was a total wreck and the other robber that had the weapon knocked out of his hand by Jolene had ran off into the woods without his weapon. Jolene was tending to Officer Brennonhan's and her wounds. Marc looked around to at the dead bodies seeing Ace's and Dice's bodies lying on the ground. However, their friend Clay had run off when the tide of battle turned.

In the meantime, back in the woods the criminal had given up looking for Deseray and decided it was time to find the truck the criminals had hidden in the woods. When he got to the truck he started to clean the leaves and the bushes off the truck. However, before he was done he felt something dripping on his head. He put his hand on top of his head then pulled it back to look at the head to find blood on it. Then he looked up to see Deseray falling from a tree with a knife pointed strait at his face. When Deseray was finally finished killing the man she searched his pockets found the keys to the car finished cleaning off the car and drove back to her dads place while still bleeding from the cuts she got from thorns, while running through the woods.

CHAPTER 15

Beauty and Pain On A River In India

"Kashmir is really beautiful," said Karina as they walked through a village in northern India. "Yes, I liked the overlooks of the rivers and valleys we saw earlier this morning," replied Michael. Michael looked over at Jolene (who was walking next to Deseray) and asked, "How did you like the trip so far?" "The area is beautiful. But I cannot wait to get to the beaches down south," Jolene said. Deseray then interrupted the conversation and said, "I am hungry let's eat."

During lunch the group ate a lot of food. Some of the foods included were lamb, rice, various vegetables, bread, and fruit. The feast was humongous. Everyone was stuffed and loved the food. No one wanted desert when offered it. Then they got on their motorcycles and headed down to Chandigarh to stay the night.

Meanwhile, in the eastern part of Indian, (between Bangladesh and Tibet) were two lovers walking down a walkway that takes you right by some waterfalls, flowers, and other rare beauty that is not seen in the United States. The two lovers were a local politician and his mistress.

Halfway down the walkway with the waterfalls they stopped and kissed. Then they continued walking until the path ended and went to an area with flowers. The man ripped the flower from the ground. Took the stem off and put the rest of the flower in his mistresses' hair. "I wonder what your wife would say if she found out we were doing this together," the woman said. "She would probably cut my nuts off," the politician replied. "Do not worry. We will never get caught," the mistress replied. Then they went to a local hotel for some afternoon fun.

When they woke up the next day Michael, Karina, and the rest of the group went out to the local market and bought some food, ate, and headed to Haridwar to tour the Hindu Holy places and see an Atari performed, but first they decided to go to New Delhi to tour the city club, dine, and have a good time for that afternoon and night.

Back in eastern India in the region of Assam the politician hooked up again with his mistress that night near a little village. The village was a nice get away spot for lovers because it was secluded and along a river so it was the perfect area because some of the houses there were a quarter to a mile or even farther away from the village. This makes the place the perfect spot to have an affair. However, this does have its disadvantages to, like not having clean drinking water at some of the houses, or many hospitals, and police nearby.

After the politician and his mistress got done trying some new sex positions, they turned the lights out and went to sleep around 1:00 AM. About an hour later they were woken up by some noise from outside in the bushes. The politician got up and walked outside with a shotgun. Then kept walking towards the bushes where the loud roars were coming from.

Out of the bushes came two Jaguars tearing a deer in half while fighting over their fresh kill. One of them chased the other away. Needing to eat the one that did not have any food turned his attention towards the politician. Then the jaguar slowly started to creep towards the politician and got into a pouncing position. At this point the politician had enough and shot the jaguar in between the eyes.

Walking back towards the house with the gun in his hand he thought to himself, "Hopefully the other Jaguar is hungry enough to eat for two because I am not going to deal with the carcass till the morning. Maybe he or she will drag the carcass off and I will not have to deal with it." After he stepped back on the porch he saw some more movement in the bushes off in another direction from the Jaguars so he went to investigate. As he walked towards the bush he was hit by a dart with a hallucinogen in it. Then he started to hallucinate that the jaguar was trying to eat him instead of the carcass. Finally, he passed out.

Waking up the next morning he noticed he was tied to a chair. A man in a black jumpsuit with gloves and a mask covering his face started to talk to him with a voice modulation device on. "So you thought you could get away with your greedy little money making scheme, didn't you? Well now you're going to pay. See you thought you could make money off the local companies by passing new environmental laws then paying off the inspectors to say the companies broke them. Then you even had one of the soft drink companies sabotaged by paying one of their employees to pour lighter fluid into some of their drinks because you own stock in another soft drink company," said the man in the black jumpsuit.

"Finally, one day the company got sued because one of the employees got a swig of it in their stomach burning their esophagus causing that employee major problems with their stomach that will last for the rest of their life. Do not worry though I work for companies fixing problems like this. First, they catch you through your paper trail or a trap. Then we take care of you whichever way the company sees fit. In this case taking you to court would not work for the company because you are part of the government which means you will be able to work your way out of it. So guess which way we picked to deal with you," continued the politician? "Oh no," the politician said! "Oh yes, the masked man replied with a smile!"

After a short pause the masked man started laughing and said, "By the way where's your mistress?" "What mistress," the politician replied? "Did you think a girl that fine would be that easy to get and keep without you spending tons of money while showing off your power to her? Don't be a fool she is just some local prostitute we paid to sleep with you and spy on you to lure you out here so I could make the kill. What did you think you were that good looking," the masked man said then started to laugh again?

When the man in the mask was done laughing he said, "Now for dramatic affect and for my amusement I have decided to cut your nuts off and drag the dead carcass of the other jaguar in here so the living one will eat you." "Please I will pay you and give you some stock in a company so you will have disposable income," the politician said crying. "Do not worry. I already have money and power. I can also take the jobs I want and I like getting rid of idiots like you who ruin the world," said the man in the mask. "The government will find you," the man in the chair said crying hysterically. In reply the hired hit man said, "Oh that is already covered. First off, there is going to be no evidence that they can get hold of they will think it is a cat that ate your manhood, which it will then it will have you for desert." Oh and by the way. If I have money and power what makes you think I do not already have clients in government," the hit man said covering the man's mouth with his hand so he could not scream.

A couple minutes later the masked man opened the front door walked over towards where the cat was finishing up the deer carcass and dragged the other jaguar's body into the house dropping the body of the cat at the castrated man's feet then he took the man's gag out of his mouth to hear him scream. Looking up and down the blood trail towards the door to see the jaguar was done with the other carcass and liking its lips. "Well looks like kitty is hungry I am going to go out the back door. I just did my good deed to help keep the habitat of this area stable by feeding kitty so I am just going out the back to let the kitty have dinner in peace," said the masked man. Then he ran out the back door. About ten yards out the back door he started to hear the screams and laughed until he heard the chopper come to pick him up in a nearby field.

Once the unmarked chopper got there the hit man jumped in and buckled up. The chopper took off. "The pilot handed him a detonator saying, "You want to do the honors?" "Yes," he replied. Then the hit man said then hit the detonator.

Suddenly, downstream from where they were a dam blew up flooding the valley and the crime scene with it. "Well that took care of it," the masked man said. "Man you're so sick how you going to cover this up," the pilot said. "We will just get our guys in the government to blame it on the other parties. I will discuss the details with you later," said the masked hit man.

Sitting in a hotel room in Haridwar Karina says, "Oh my God with," with a look of horror on her face as she sees that the dam has exploded and the Prime Minister of India takes to the podium to speak on the telivision. "Ok, shut that off. Nothing is going to ruin our vacation like it almost did in Brazil so stop worrying about it. They will still have the Atari tonight. Let's go out and enjoy ourselves," Michael said annoyed as he turned the TV off.

Upon stepping outside the doors of the hotel Karina asked, "Where are Jolene and Deseray?" Michael answered, "At the pool inside the hotel. Jolene is obsessed with getting Deseray another man other than the lame sauce she has at home." Karina shook her head and replied, "Jolene needs to give it up. After what happened to Paul she has decided to stick with someone who is cautious and does not like to travel a lot, or do crazy stuff like Paul did. "What about the guy at the club," said Michael? "She did like going repelling off of cliffs and sky diving with Paul. I remember her telling me stories about it. The guy at the club was the same way. Well let's go down to the markets by the Ganges River and enjoy the day," replied Karina.

Walking through the market Karina and Michael saw many things that caught their attention. Michael bought a watch with diamonds in it and Karina bought a Red Bandhani printed Sari to wear at the Atari. After shopping they ate at a local snack bar and walked off the food they ate. As they walked along the Ganges Karina asked, "What is going on over there? Why is everybody in wearing white on the river? What is up with the big fire and ceremony?" The couple walked a little farther down the river. Then they saw another couple standing watching the ceremony and asked what the ceremony was about. The answer they got was it was a Hindu funeral and they were cremating the body. They continued to watch the funeral and went back to the hotel.

That night Jolene, Deseray, Michael, and Karina went to the Atari along the Ganges River. At the Atari they watched the singing, the idols, and the God's. They also took in the aroma of the incense, and took in the sights of the beautiful flowers as well as the costumes. After the lighting of the flames they went clubbing.

At the club Jolene and Deseray spent most of the time on the dance floor. On the other hand, Michael and Karina did some dancing but spent most of their time drinking at a table. After a while Michael and Karina got tired and went back to the hotel.

Meanwhile, Jolene and Deseray continued to dance late into the night. One of the guys that Jolene was dancing with stole her wallet out of her purse and went into the bathroom. Deseray saw it and told Jolene. The man a couple of minutes later came out of the bathroom and walked out the side door of the club into an alley where a car was with two men waiting for him. Jolene pulled a knife she had hidden on her thigh and walked outside slashing the two back tires of the car. All three of the men got out of the car and one of them said, "You made a big mistake little girl." Then tried to slap Jolene upside the face but before his hand connected Jolene slapped his hand out of the way and broke his nose. The other two idiots tried to attack Deseray but she pulled a knife on the one and grabbed him by the arm slicing an artery in his wrist then kicked him in the stomach knocking him on the ground.

Deseray pointed the knife at the other man that had a broken nose and he as well as his friend ran away. Jolene pulled some cuffs out of her purse and cuffed the guy with the slight wrist to the car door. Then sorted through his pockets as well as the car and found her wallet.

After that she took a lighter and lit his wallet on fire. Everything burned except for his ID that she had taken out of the wallet. Then she looked behind her to notice a dog eating out of the dumpster. With a smile on her face she threw to the dog what was left of the wallet and the dog chewed up what was left of the wallet swallowing it whole. Then they called the police. When the police finally arrived they gave their testimony and left.

The next day the group of all four of them checked out of their hotel. Grabbed a bite to eat then they went to New Delhi to catch their flight to Goa. The rest of the week they spent on their vacation they hung out at the local beaches, as well as the night clubs, went snorkeling, and sightseeing at the temples.

CHAPTER 16

Condemnation, Loose Ends And Forgiveness

John and Janet Lieberum were driving cross country on a 105 degree day across Kansas. The air conditioner was broke down so they were driving with the windows down. "I cannot wait to see Oregon again," said Janet. "Yes, and I cannot wait till the sun goes down. To get out of this sun and the wind burn we are getting looks weird too," replied John. "The sun is making me tired let's switch and you can drive at the next town."

Eighty miles later, the Lieberums pulled into a rest station in a town of 500 people. A man is filling up his pickup truck to go do farm work. John asks the man, "So what is there to do around here?" "Nothing just farming," he replied. "Do you like it here," John said asking yet another question? "No, it is boring. I wish I lived in another state," he replied. "At least there are nice people here," John stated. "Yeah, that's true," said the man.

Meanwhile, Janet had filled up the gas tank and walked into the gas station to get something to drink. "There is a blond seventeen year old working at the counter (or talking on her cell more than working). Janet starts looking around at all the snacks and walks down an aisle to overhear the little girl at the counter talking bad about her. Telling her friends over the phone how dumb she was because she thought Janet was taking a long time getting her food. Then Janet thought to herself, Ok, I will show her. She grabbed a candy bar and a sports drink, walked up to the counter threw the candy bar down on the counter so it slid to the edge of the counter on the girl's side. The girl then says to her friend on the phone. "Hold on one second and let me put the phone down on the counter. I got a customer." "The candy bar and the drink," Janet said while drinking a little of the soft drink. Then she put the drink down on the counter and knocked it over onto the girl's phone. Quickly Janet picked it up before all the sports drink could make it out of the bottle to make it look like it was an accident. Then Janet said, "I am sorry you got any towels and some cleaner let me clean it up." "No I got it," the girl replied! After the girl had cleaned up the mess she ran Janet's items through the register and Janet paid. Upon leaving the store Janet got in the passenger side of the vehicle John put the car into drive and pulled out of the gas station.

Later, on down the road Janet fell asleep while John was listening to a pastor on the radio. The pastor read from James Chapter 2 starting in verse 20.

James 2 [20] You foolish person, do you want evidence that faith without deeds is useless? [21] Was not our father Abraham considered righteous for what he did when he offered his son Isaac on the altar? [22] You see that his faith and his actions were working together, and his faith was made complete by what he did. [23] And the scripture was fulfilled that says, "Abraham believed God, and it was credited to him as righteousness," and he was called God's friend. [24] You see that a person is considered righteous by what they do and not by faith alone. [25] In the same way, was not even Rahab the prostitute considered righteous for what she did when she gave lodging to the spies and sent them off in a different direction? [26] As the body without the spirit is dead, so faith without deeds is dead (NIV)."

Meanwhile, back in the small town in Kansas the seventeen year old girl from the gas station was driving down the highway to a party with a bunch of her drunken friends in the car with her. Her boyfriend is sitting in the car drinking a beer next to her. He leans over to try to kiss her she says, "Get a mint," and then takes her hand putting it in his face to push him away. Suddenly, a text message comes on her phone. Next, her friend texted her about the party she was hosting and was asking in the when they would be there? The seventeen year old texted back, "In ten minutes," and then looks up to see that she had crossed over the yellow line in the road. Her car collided with a pizza delivery boy's car and every one dies except for one of the passengers and the delivery boy who is medevac'd to the hospital.

Two weeks later the Lieberums are driving back from their vacation down the same stretch of highway where the seventeen year old and all of her friends died except for one. There is also a memorial for the girl on the side of the road. Janet looking concerned tells John to pull off the highway and into the town so they can get a paper.

Walking into the same gas station as the last time, Janet grabbed something to drink, and a paper. The paper had on the front page "Home Coming Queen Dead in Car Accident, Three Others Killed, Two Injured." The article went on to explain how she was a cheerleader. Her boyfriend was captain of the football team. There was also alcohol and texting involved. To add to the horror the town made a memorial in her name. On the back page in an even smaller block was an article about the pizza boy who was in the same accident and how he was now in a wheel chair for life. All that Janet had to say to the incident was, "Only here in the United States could we celebrate irresponsibility with a memorial in the name of the person committing the crime."

Meanwhile, back in Pennsylvania Jolene walked out the police department in uniform as Jake walked by. As soon as Jake saw her he said, "I knew there was something wrong with you and you were too good to be true. I cannot believe you." "Look hun, I am only saying this because you need to know the truth about yourself. Obviously, no one has told you this or they have and you were not listening. You need to stop womanizing and being a jerk. I know what I did was ignorant and I am sorry for it. However, you really need to grow up and act like a man. Otherwise you will never have a successful relationship. Good Bye," said Jolene. Then she walked away from him. Jake just stood there looking dumb founded as she walked away.

Later on that night Jake left from work at the gym and went out to eat with Brad and Tatiana. After they were done eating they went clubbing. Jake just sat down drinking and thinking about what Jolene had just said to him.

Brad and Tatiana spent most of the night on the dance floor. In the meantime Jane walked into the club with her new boyfriend. Great, there's another mistake in my life that shows up again, Jake thought to himself.

Noticing something was wrong Brad came back to the table and said, "What's up?" "I saw Jolene today and found out she was a cop. Then she told me I was a jerk and everything," Jake said. "Well, I knew that a long time ago Jake," replied Brad. "Well why didn't you say anything," Jake asked? "No one ever listens to anyone else when it comes to love. Especially their friends because the friends are the third party that are not in the relationship so they can see the good and the bad in the relationship. The two in love are normally blind to the other person's faults or choose to ignore them to make the relationship work. When they finally pull their head from their rear and figure out that it will never work it is usually too late they are married, have kids, being cheated on, or something. Why else do you think most marriages do not work? Other than people do not try anymore because with a no fault divorce they can just say; we grew apart, we did not work out, were just two different people or my personal favorite. I thought he/she would change after we got married or had kids. Get real! If they are not ready to be a good spouse or parent before they are married the odds of them changing are slim afterwards. Most the time they never change. The worst part about the situation the kids are the ones that are hurt the most. Look, this is a learning experience you are a Christian. God forgave everything you did past, present, and future through Christ's death on the cross so quit acting like you are going to burn in hell for the way you have lived your life and move on. Only losers give up and quit acting all emasculated it looks pathetic," he said and started to laugh at Jake. Jake cracked a smile and said, "You know your right." Then Jake went to the dance floor and found someone to dance with.

A month later, Jane's relationship with her new boyfriend has run its course. Jake went to the club with Brad, Tatiana, and Jane. This time Karina, Michael, Deseray, and Jolene show up also. Deseray says to Jolene, out on the dance floor. "Look how cute Jane is here and with Jake." "Maybe he actually listened to what I said," said Jolene. "No he is too stupid for that," said Deseray and they both broke out into laughter.

Jake and Jane danced together most of the night then Jane left. Finally, Jake sat down with Brad and Tatiana talking as while the others dance. After a couple of minutes talking Jake noticed that three guys had been around since around the same time Deseray had walked in. They had been watching her most the night. Michael and Katrina had left. Brad kissed Tatiana good bye and walked her to her car. Jolene left sick earlier so it was only Jake and Deseray there. Jake walked up to Deseray who was at the bar getting a drink and told Deseray that he would like to walk her out to her car because three guys were watching her. She replied, "Get lost and he walked back to his seat." Deseray called her boyfriend on the phone, who worked night shift at his new job. Jake continued to watch the other guys who were still watching her. Deseray, stayed there a few more hours and so did the guys. Finally, she left but so did the guys. Jake followed them into the parking lot as Deseray pulled out. A car pulled up and the driver of the car whose face was too far away to see yelled, "Get in," to the guys following Deseray and they chased after her! Jake followed suit.

After following for fifteen minutes Jake decided to call the police. In reply to all the information he gave the police they said we will have an officer on the way keep on the phone. Just then the people following Deseray pulled off the road Jake told the police that they were no longer following her but they replied, "The license plate number of the car he was following was stolen and that police were on their way out." After taking his number they told him that they were hanging up and to make sure he made it home safe. Then they thanked him for his help as they hung up the phone. Deseray was still in front of him and Jake continued to follow her to make sure she made it home safe.

Deseray's phone started to ring but just as she went to answer it the men following her earlier came down a side street and hit her car with their car almost knocking her off the road. Then Jake plowed them from behind with his car flipping theirs. Deseray's car engine went dead and Jake pulled up to her and yelling, "Get in"!!! She slowly got out of her car pulling out her handgun and ran for Jake's car. Then they speed away. "Go to my house I will call my dad and he will show up with the police, let me borrow your phone." Deseray tried to call her dad but they were out of cell range. Do not worry; I have a shot gun at home you can use if there are more of them when we get there.

When they pulled up to the house Jolene called her and was able to get through. Deseray said, "Jolene," in a loud voice. "What is wrong," Jolene replied? "Those guys tried to finish me off this time. Please call my dad and get the police to my house." "Do not worry we will be there shortly someone already called us," said Jolene then hung up.

When Deseray and Jake pulled up to the house, they cautiously walked in the back door with Deseray pulling her gun out of the holster. After they opened the door Deseray and Jake went down to where her rifles were locked up. She gave Jake one and grabbed one herself. She also went and grabbed a large knife and handed Jake one to. A couple seconds later the lights went out and two men in masks with jump suits as well as armored plated vests on broke through the windows.

After they broke through the windows the people in jumpsuits started shooting at them with automatic weapons. Jake and Deseray dove behind the couch then popped up shooting them both in the chest. The guys fell back onto the floor Deseray and Jake approached one cautiously. When Jake went to pull the mask off of one of them and the man tried to stab Jake but Jake shot him in the head. The other one got up and ran out of the room. Deseray shoot at the man and missed. They inspected the body of the man on the floor noticing the armored plated vest and cyanide pills on him. "She turned to Jake and said, "Were in deep crap now. No one brings cyanide pills unless they are told to get the job done or do not come back. If they are caught talking to the police or come back Mr. Indescribable will probably have their family killed."

Just then, more gunmen flew through the window Jake and Deseray shoot them both in the head sending them crashing dead to the floor. The other man they did not kill earlier came around the corner shooting at them and missed. Then he hid back behind the corner in the hallway they were in. They rushed towards him shooting down the hallway and he popped behind the corner to shoot at them but Deseray threw her knife at him hitting him right in the gut.

Meanwhile, the police showed up on the property but and rocket came out of the woods taking out the first cop car then a slew of bullets came out of the woods too. The police retreated and called for backup. Deseray and Jake saw the cop car burning outside the window and Deseray called her dad to see if he was all right. Marc answered, "Deseray I am ok and I see the cop car. We are going to come in through the woods with an S.W.A.T. team to take out the snipers. Do not try to come outside there are snipers on the roof. Try to hold them off until Jolene comes up through the woods and sets up a sniper position to take the heat off of you."

Just then more gunmen came through the windows. One knocked Jake on the ground and three others started shooting at Deseray. Jake tripped the one trying to kill him and knocked him on the ground while Deseray killed the others. Jake was still rolling around fighting the man on the ground when Deseray pulled out her handgun and shoot the guy in the head.

After they were all killed Deseray and Jake started to hear some fire being exchanged between the police and the gunmen outside. Then one of the gunmen fell off the roof outside onto the ground and died. A phone call came in on Jake's phone from Deseray's dad saying Jolene is in position but do not try to leave because we still have not gotten rid of the criminal with the rocket propelled grenade launcher but we know where he is and are bringing a helicopter to take care of it so hold them off. There are a bunch of them on the roof and Jolene has got them pinned down.

Then suddenly a bomb went off and Deseray and Jake threw themselves to the ground. The basement door was kicked open and a smoke grenade was thrown from the basement onto the floor. Then more gunmen started flowing out of the basement. Deseray and Jake picked up the guns from the dead bodies on the ground to begin shooting at some of them. A couple of them had made it out of the basement without begin shot the rest laid dead on the floor. When the smoke cleared another gunmen fell off the roof. Then Deseray and Jake pushed forward, trying to clear the house of the gunmen. As they walked past the living room three gunmen popped up from behind the couch and two from one of the bedrooms down the hallway. Diving forward into the hallway with the two gunmen that popped out of the bedroom Deseray and Jake shoot them both killing them. Then they ran into the bedroom grabbing one of the guy's bodies and dragging it in to poach it of weapons. Then they shut the door behind them.

Deseray and Jake started poaching the bodies. They found two grenades and a smoke grenade. Then Deseray said, "Ok there's three of them first we will shoot the door open then throw the smoke grenade and charge out there kill those three and throw a grenade down the stairs of the basement so no more can come up through there on the count of three."

Deseray started to count but before she could say three a gunman broke through the window of the bedroom and they killed them, shot the door open then threw a smoke grenade out as they charged out the room. Deseray killed the three more gunmen as Jake threw the grenade down the basement stairs taking out the stairs. Then they heard a chopper above them and a chain gun start shooting and bodies started falling off the roof. The gun fire started to die down a little outside. They started to make their way for the back door. However, when passing one of the closets, the closet flew open and a gunman tried to shot Deseray but Jake threw himself in front of her taking the bullet. Deseray turned around and shoot the man in the midsection and started dragging Jake who was bleeding badly towards the door.

However, Deseray and Jake never made it outside because the helicopter after taking out the men on the roof drew the attention of the man in the woods with the rocket propelled grenade launcher. The man took aim and fired sending the helicopter which was over top the roof crashing into the house. The roof caved in on both Deseray and Jake.

After coming back from their trip out west the Lieberums sat down and relaxed. Janet went out to tan outside while John sat and read the Bible. He read:

1 John 1:5 – "In the beginning was the Word, and the Word was with God, and the Word was God. [2] He was with God in the beginning.[3] Through him all things were made; without him nothing was made that has been made. [4] In him was life, and that life was the light of all mankind. [5] The light shines in the darkness, and the darkness has not overcome it. [6] There was a man sent from God whose name was John. [7] He came as a witness to testify concerning that light, so that through him all might believe. [8] He himself was not the light; he came only as a witness to the light (NIV)."

Then he read Luke 6:32- "If you love those who love you, what credit is that to you? Even sinners love those who love them.[33] And if you do good to those who are good to you, what credit is that to you? Even sinners do that.[34] And if you lend to those from whom you expect repayment, what credit is that to you? Even sinners lend to sinners, expecting to be repaid in full. [35] But love your enemies, do good to them, and lend to them without expecting to get anything back. Then your reward will be great, and you will be children of the Most High, because he is kind to the ungrateful and wicked. [36] Be merciful, just as your Father is merciful (NIV)."

[43] "No good tree bears bad fruit, nor does a bad tree bear good fruit. [44] Each tree is recognized by its own fruit. People do not pick figs from thorn bushes, or grapes from briers. [45] A good man brings good things out of the good stored up in his heart, and an evil man brings evil things out of the evil stored up in his heart. For the mouth speaks what the heart is full of (NIV)." This brought a tear to John's eye.

Later, that night John kissed his wife good night then rolled over in bed and turned the light off. Janet fell asleep easily but he could not so early in the morning he decided to go to Pennsylvania and left a note to his wife explaining why.

When John got to Pennsylvania he walked in the police station where Marc worked at and asked to talk to Detective Skylark. Marc walked him into his office told him to have a seat and shut the door.

Later, that night Deseray woke up from a coma with Marc sitting by her side. Marc smiled and said, "I have some good news and some bad news." "What is it," she replied? "We found Paul's killer but it is not Jake," answered Marc. "He saved my life back at the house so I figured he did not do it. Who is it and where is Jake," replied Deseray? Jake is still in a coma and the killer was Michael's uncle John Lieburum. He confessed to everything including killing other people around the world but it's a long story you get some sleep and I will tell you later," Marc answered?

Later, that night Marc explained to Deseray the story while walking her in a wheel chair down the hallway to Jake's room:

Uncle Lieburum walked into my office and told me he was the killer and also did a lot of killings on different continents. He told me about killing Paul and how he dumped the murder weapon, the pipe in the New York City Harbor. I asked him why he did that and he said, "Paul was a hypocrite. Part of my job as a private eye was to do surveillance of on people who were thought to be cheating by their spouses and bring them any information that would prove their infidelity. In one of my cases five years ago, I ran into a guy who was sleeping with my friend's wife. I showed my friend the pictures and needless to say a week later there was an agreement signed for a divorce. The wife got only a car because not only was she sleeping with another man she was also sleeping around with a supervisor at work and we had the pictures, which meant she would loss in court."

"My friend became depressed and tried dating but the girls only wanted him for his money or as an emotional dump, so he decided to live alone. We would talk on the phone every once in a while and everything seemed to be fine. However, one time he called and he was crying because he said he felt so alone. I told him to go join a church bible study group or a singles group at church and do some activities with them so he would not have to be alone. A couple days later I called and he did not answer. Then I called again two days later and no answer so I went to the house to find him dead on the floor with sleeping pills on his dresser drawer," said John to me.

John continued his story by saying, "Later, at Michael and Karina's wedding I saw the guy that was sleeping with his wife again and that is where I found out his name, "Paul," so I wanted to right the wrongs that he had committed by killing him." After his confession I asked him, why he wrote hypocrite on the wall. John said, "I knew Paul was a Christian and he was sleeping with another person's wife."

Deseray asked, "Since Uncle Lieberum was obviously following Paul around to plan the murder did he know whether Paul was cheating on me while we were together?" I asked the same question being concerned for you Deseray and Uncle Lieberum, said, "No and that he does not look back on the day of Paul's death without regret. He said, "I feel bad and that Paul had really changed because he never cheated on you when he was following him. I really wished I would have thought about that people can change and I would have never killed him that night. I read the bible and that made me realize I was the one being a real hypocrite by not forgiving. That's why I turned myself in."

"After that John went on to tell him how he killed a women in Venice for sleeping around on her husband called Mrs. Rossi using a chemicals in a fur coat that burned her after the chemical reacted to her sweat and made her jump into the water where he drowned her. He also said he had drugged the man in the devils mask and her at the masquerade ball they were at," Marc said.

Later on, John said, "When the two headed to the hotel Mrs. Rossi walked ahead of the man in the devils mask and around the corner of one of the back alleys of Venice. In the back alley is where I stepped in and jumped him stealing his clothes as well as his mask then I followed her back to the hotel and using coliform on her to knock her out. From there you know rest of the story." "To verify he was not lying, he told me that at the crime scene he wrote "whore," on the sidewalk because she was with her husband for just money which obviously makes her a whore because the odds are very good if you are married you are having sex with him or her," said Marc.

"Then Uncle Lieberium told me about two more killings," Two more replied Deseray," with a look of concern on her face. Then after a pause she said, "I never would have thought that he was that way when I talked to him. What other sick things did he do," asked Deseray?

"Well, later on he went up to the mountains to check up on his wife at a ski resort in Italy, up in the Dolomites. Killing a young girl named Maria with poisonous spiders from Africa.

The reason he did this is because she had stock in an American oil company that has to give bribes to people in the Russian mafia to do business without interruption so workers do not end up missing if the company did not do what the mafia wanted. On top of this the cigarette company she invested in purposely puts more nicotine and even a little antifreeze (for flavor) in their cigarettes to get people addicted (not for the flavor like they say) and causes many more people to get cancer than the average cigarette," Marc told Deseray. Then Marc stopped pushing Deseray in the hallway to look out the hospital window at the flowers blooming with a couple of butterflies flying around them bringing a pause to the conversation as well as a smile to both of their faces.

Continuing their walk toward Jakes room, Marc started to tell the rest of the story. "In his final killing John killed an important political figure in India for stealing from some of the companies in India tying him up and using a dead jaguars carcass to attract another one to eat the politician. One of the companies he worked with got smart to the schemes he would run and caught him through the paper trail he left behind him. They found out he was paying inspector's money to fail companies on new environmental laws (that he would help pass) so they could sue them to get more money in his political party for elections, projects, and his own personal account. He even went as far as to sabotage a company. One that he worked for that his old company competed against so that later when he got out of politics he would go back to his old company. Then he would make millions more because of less competitive competition. This would make him the scum of all politicians (at least in India). The only problem is I have nothing to try him on that murder because he took care of the evidence with blowing a dam so there is no jaguar, or body to be found. The Indian government cannot find the body or carcass anywhere so the case will remain a missing person's case. Another problem was that the bomb was a homemade one with no traces back to John so I cannot even try him on the deaths of the countless people he killed in the ensuing flood cause by the dam blowing up."

"Well it looks like they all deserved it except for Paul. John was really trying to take care of some real bad people. I do not see why he could justify Paul's death by someone committing suicide over a wife? No human is worth that much grief so why did he kill all these people? What was his ultimate goal," replied Deseray just as they got to the door of the room Jake was in? "Well he justified it by using James 1:27 in the bible, "27 Religion that God our Father accepts as pure and faultless is this: to look after orphans and widows in their distress and to keep oneself from being polluted by the world (NIV)." Think about it. His friend kills himself because of another man and his wife cheating. Therefore, due to seeing the pain that individual was put through, he decided to right the wrongs of the world and play God himself which, that is where John Lieberium said that he went wrong. The reason he turned himself in was because he realized from reading passages like Luke 6:32- "If you love those who love you, what credit is that to you? Even sinners love those who love them.33 And if you do good to those who are good to you, what credit is that to you? Even sinners do that.34 And if you lend to those from whom you expect repayment, what credit is that to you? Even sinners lend to sinners, expecting to be repaid in full. 35 But love your enemies, do good to them, and lend to them without expecting to get anything back. Then your reward will be great, and you will be children of the Most High, because he is kind to the ungrateful and wicked. 36 Be merciful, just as your Father is merciful (NIV)."

At this point the conversation stopped and they entered the room to see Jake asleep in a coma. They prayed for Jake and went back to their conversation. Marc pulled out the bible in the cabinet next to the bed and showed Deseray 1 John chapter 4 and read part of the chapter to her. "John said that these passages and other passages convicted him that he was not living like Jesus wanted him to and love one another as Jesus did. He realized this and asked Jesus to be his savior after reading this passage [13]"This is how we know that we live in him and he in us: He has given us of his Spirit. [14] And we have seen and testify that the Father has sent his Son to be the Savior of the world. [15] If anyone acknowledges that Jesus is the Son of God, God lives in them and they in God. [16] And so we know and rely on the love God has for us. God is love. Whoever lives in love lives in God, and God in them. [17] This is how love is made complete among us so that we will have confidence on the day of judgment: In this world we are like Jesus. [18] There is no fear in love. But perfect love drives out fear, because fear has to do with punishment. The one who fears is not made perfect in love.[19] We love because he first loved us. [20] Whoever claims to love God yet hates a brother or sister is a liar. For whoever does not love their brother and sister, whom they have seen, cannot love God, whom they have not seen. [21] And he has given us this command: Anyone who loves God must also love their brother and sister (NIV)."

"This is why we need to read our bible and be in the word so we do not take one part of the bible and turn the part into something it was not intended to be. Sure we are not going to let a baby, a widow or the poor suffer, even if we have to protect them in a violent way which means war is horrible but if they're going to kill our own children in their beds then doing nothing about that would be just as evil if not worse that is why people who kill someone at war do not get prosecuted for this except under extenuated circumstances. God is good so he is not going to send someone to hell for defending an innocent baby or a minority group.

Meanwhile, Jesus does want us to ultimately give up everything even oneself or children even if that means no retaliation. That God considers the best way. Think about all those pastors who were killed but did not fight back does not that show one is stronger than others. It is by far harder to sit back and let someone hurt you or your family so it will be looked at as a higher sacrifice in heaven then actually defending one's self or family. Both are good choices though in the end because God is good and one shows obedience to God while the other is still following his law in James 1:27. Why would God send his own son to die then isn't that the most ultimate sacrifice as well as bad? No it is not. God saw it as righteousness that Abraham would listen to his God and want to sacrifice his son for him but since that is a sin that would not be good so he let Abraham's son live.

However, because no amount of sacrifices like lambs could make up for all the sins of the world or even his own people which by the time of their exile to Babylon were doing the most despicable acts like sacrificing ones children to other gods or just sacrificing them in general so God's plan from the beginning was to have one sacrifice for all sins past, present, and future his son who did nothing wrong being the perfect sacrifice. He had to have been perfect because if not like a lamb that was not the best of the flock God would not accept the sacrifice. This means Jesus could not have sinned at all or if you do not believe he was the perfect sacrifice by being perfect then to you he died for nothing."

"Good argument but would not someone say sacrificing their child is evil therefore God is evil," said Deseray. "Well you know how the angels are amazed by some of the things God lets people do that angels cannot get away with it. I think they are most amazed at God's choice of letting people have free will and get mercy when they do something wrong. God did not make people to be robots and follow his every command what would the point of that be, because the angles already have to do that and that is not free will. People, who do not have to follow but still choose to by following God, also prove his power to the angles, and the devil that I think is what's truly astonishing. Like the story of Job. Where even after all of that pain and suffering he went through he still praised God. God has to be good which means everyone has to be punished for what they do wrong whether the punishment comes here or in the afterlife. Free will means there has to be consequences to our actions otherwise if there are no consequences, who would do good, and that would mean God is not good? Therefore, a world with no motivation to do good by not having consequences cannot be good and that God would be wrong, as well as evil in doing so. God is also supposed to be perfect so why would he make a world that has no consequences. That would be making the world bad intentionally, which makes no sense," said Marc.

"We may not even see the consequences in some cases. For instance, think what would happen if a person picked the right action. Maybe they might get something good in return but in this case they did not. The reason is there could be more than one right action but they did not pick the best one. Therefore, they did not receive as good of a reward as they could have. There are also multiple actions that are not good choices but there are also choices that can be even more detrimental. Therefore, the consequences might not be as dire as they could have been," replied Marc ending the conversation. Then after spending some time next to Jake's bed with Jake not waking up, Marc took Karina back to her room so she could sleep and left.

SIX MONTHS LATER

After a short court case John Lieberum pleaded guilty to four counts of first degree murder with the sentence of death. Deseray forgave him and asked for life in prison. However, the families of the other victims wanted him dead so he got lethal injection instead. One mystery went unsolved though John never admitted to kidnapping or killing Christian and there was no evidence to stick to him, so there was no charge brought against him for that crime and the killer is still on the loose.

Next, Maria the bank teller got married to Martin Benin. Then the same pizza delivery boy who caused the fatal accident down at the beach in North Carolina was speeding again. However, this time after a long day at work he fell asleep at the wheel and drove off the road into the water. He was able to swim out of the car but when he started to swim to shore fins circled around him and he was pulled down into the water.

Derick's dog ended up getting neutered and the Persian cat did get impregnated by the Russian Blues cat ruining their Persian pure breed cat. Finally, Jake did recover and begged Jane for forgiveness. She took him back and a year later dumbed him saying she had grown tired of him. A month later she started dating a stock broker and moved to his Manhattan penthouse suit. Jane she would eventually marry the stock broker.

A year later Deseray was sitting on a beach in South Africa watching the sun set as the moon began to rise into the sky at the same time. Sitting next to her was Jake holding her hand. Then she leaned over to him and kissed him.

THE END